THE
BRIDE WHO
RAN AWAY

THE
BRIDE WHO
RAN AWAY

DIANA O'HEHIR

CHATTO & WINDUS

LONDON

This book was completed with the help of generous financial grants from the Guggenheim Foundation and the National Endowment for the Arts and with the provision of working space, time, and encouragement by Ragdale Foundation and, many times over, by MacDowell Colony.

Published in 1988 by
Chatto & Windus Ltd
30 Bedford Square
London WC1B 3RP

First published by Atheneum 1988

A CIP catalogue record for this book is available from the British Library.

ISBN 0 7011 3297 3

Printed in Great Britain by
Redwood Burn Ltd, Trowbridge, Wiltshire

For Mel

1

Sybil and I were discussing Disastrous Attachments. "A Disastrous Attachment is one that makes you feel worse instead of better," she said. "How does Steve make you feel?"

I didn't answer her.

"You have to break loose from a Disastrous Attachment. May I sit down?"

Sybil was eighty-three years old, and was my great-aunt. I reached up to steady her while she edged onto the step of the French Ford General Store, where I had been sitting reading a letter.

"What do you want with those cans of motor oil?" I asked her. Sybil has sounded coherent during this conversation, but she had moments of dislocation, and one thing she did during those moments was to steal from the General Store anything she could grab during a swift trip inside the door. She was carrying a green net bag that held three pry-open cans of Pennzoil.

Sybil wore a pink tweed suit with a velvet collar, a black

1

cashmere sweater, one yellow glass earring and one silver one. Her white hair was drawn back in a bun. The only immediately odd thing about her was the winter clothing—the temperature was over ninety today—but a close observer might also have noticed the earrings, and an even closer one the seamed cotton stockings. "Where *does* she get them?" my cousin Indiana asked. "There *are* no stockings like that any more; she must have a hoard somewhere." When Indiana said this I speculated about the space under the back seat of Sybil's Buick, or maybe about a cupboard deep in the rubbish hill, beneath the pattern of rocks and tin cans.

Sybil lived in her car, a high tan one with a mahogany dashboard which sat on a hill in the diggings outside town. The ground there had been washed clean by hydraulic mining and was striped gray, purple, and green; small manzanita bushes grew among the gravel.

"You have a letter from Steve." She had recognized Steve's handwriting; he was my cousin and her great-nephew.

Carissima, Steve wrote, *how am I supposed to tell you about it? Don't ask. No, of course I don't love you the way I've loved before . . . Every love is different . . .*

"It is none of my business, but I simply have *questions*," Sybil persisted. "I do not think that marriage will work."

I squeezed Steve's letter to make it crackle.

Surely you will someday understand.

Everything about me.

I squinted at Sybil, whose severe white head had surrounded itself with a silver nimbus. Perhaps I didn't want to understand everything about Steve.

There is a French philosopher who says the greatest

2

good is to betray your best friend. Do you agree, Grazia? No, I thought you might not.

I folded the letter and put it down the front of my jeans. "Let's go for a walk."

Sybil attached herself to my outstretched arm and maneuvered herself up. "The thing I like least about him is his didactic tone. Like your dentist."

"Sybil," I said, "what a weird family we are."

Sybil was the ultimate extreme of which the Dowells were capable, but all of us—all my Dowell aunts, uncles, and cousins—had her daffy possibility. "Stark raving bats," my cousin Indiana had said, standing in front of her mirror, combing her long blonde hair. Indiana was a Dowell, too. She sucked in her waist and admired her six nylon petticoats. "I'm going to San Francisco and be a dancer."

Sybil and I were now crossing Fifth Avenue. French Ford had no First, Second, Third, or Fourth avenues, only a Fifth; maybe the original Gold Rush settlers had hoped that the magic name would bring them an instant New York sophistication. Fifth Avenue was unpaved and had on it Mrs. Farmer's yellow-painted wide-porched house with the peach orchard. We walked up Fifth Avenue slowly; Sybil flexed her arthritic hand to make a shadow on the red dust and talked about my wedding. "I suppose it will be an elegant event." At the top of Fifth Avenue there was a horse-trough, a pump, and a wooden bench with a plaque on it memorializing my great-grandmother, "a fighter for truth." We sat on the bench for a few minutes and then started back down toward Main Street and my father's house.

We had the nicest house in French Ford, a high white

one with a wide front porch, tall narrow windows, graceful cornices. Daddy had inherited the house from my
grandparents; it looked like the *National Geographic* pho-
tographs of New England, but I didn't think French Ford's
sharp blue air and herbal smell could much resemble New
England.

Sybil and I crossed the porch, avoiding the branches of
the elm tree, and headed for the wooden swing. We sat
down on that, I in one corner and she in the other; I began
to rock us back and forth by pushing with one foot. The
roof of the porch creaked; catty-corner across Main Street,
in his dark red cottage, our drunken neighbor made a
muffled noise with his pots. From the top of a hill behind
the church a radio blurted loudly. Except for the radio and
our neighbor French Ford was silent; there were no car
noises, the heat overlay the setting in a blue blanket.

Idly I observed that the only fragment of motion over
the town was a scrap of disturbed atmosphere—the kind
you got from running your household heat in the wintertime—that hovered over the far end of Main Street in the
spot where Indiana's yellow shingle house was.

Sybil was talking about Napa State Hospital for the
Insane. The hardest thing, she said, was the meals. "You
had to have all your meals with those people. And they
were crazy."

"What kind of crazy?"

"They were all women. It was a women's wing."

The psychology books I had been reading suggested that
I might feel guilty about Sybil's stay in Napa—she had
gone there after she kidnapped me. We were missing for a
week before my father found us living in the university's

experimental mine. But I was only two at that time, and I didn't think I felt guilty. "They talked about clay," Sybil said.

Clay. I fished for the right question. Sticky clay, Sybil? The clay out of the Bible? It was hard sometimes to discover what Sybil was aiming at.

The porch roof groaned rhythmically. From the dark red cottage there was a clatter and an exclamation, which I interpreted as "sonuvvabitch." Suddenly, over these sounds, over my thoughts, occurred a brief shiver in the air like a giant alarm clock. Sybil and I put our hands over our ears. The French Ford fire siren had gone off.

Our siren equipment had been bought from the city of Sacramento after the war. Here in French Ford it was supposed to summon the members of the volunteer fire department from their jobs around town or down at the dam. My cousin Indiana said the siren noise was one you could hear with your teeth.

I scrambled to stand on the swing, hold on to the chains, stare out over the town. I could see the roof of the firehouse, its yellow back wall, the siren on it seeming, I thought, to send out visible circles of sound. I saw two men burst out the door of the General Store and lope around the corner to the firehouse; I saw a green P G and E truck skid up out of Quarry Pit Road with two men in the cab and three more in the flatbed.

"There's no smoke," I said. The siren wound down to an insect mutter.

There was a pause. The back firehouse door came up; the truck backed out, turned around, kicking dust and gravel haze, and drove half a block up the street, where it stopped in front of Indiana's house. On Indiana's front porch a figure in a print dress gestured. All the windows of the house were shut.

Sybil was too old to run; the most she could manage was a dignified hobble. I held her hand and tried not to pull; I even stopped to tuck a shred of her white hair back into its bun. "What do you think it is?" I asked. "Oh, Sybil, what do you think?" The question was ridiculous; asking it gave me something to do.

Main Street's course, until it passed the General Store, was downhill in the shade; after that the road turned a corner and went uphill through sun. Sybil began to walk unevenly; we had to stop and sit on the seamstress's front porch. The seamstress was not there; like everyone else in French Ford she had followed the fire engine. But she had left her screen door unhooked and I went into her kitchen and got Sybil a glass of water. I ran the water for a while over my wrists and fingers; then I ran water into the glass to cool the glass; then I asked myself how much of this was a means of postponing our arrival at Indiana's house.

"I told you no good would come of your engagement," Sybil said as I handed her the glass. I sat beside her and put my hands around my knees.

Indiana's house was only eight doors off now; the sounds from there were subdued, an indistinct crowd murmur, as of people saying: oh my, or oh dear. Underneath that there was the throb of a machine. I lowered my head onto my knees. Sybil drank her glass of water and put one arm around me. "There," she said, approaching the corner of her shoulder to my forehead; "there, now." She smelled peculiar but not unpleasant, dusty and mineral, like the diggings in the sun.

It was half an hour before we finally reached Indiana's house and pushed our way past the crowd on the front porch and through the tiny parlor into the kitchen. Indiana lay in the middle of her kitchen floor, surrounded by swirls and patterns and footprints of blood, a litter of paper napkins, stained towels, rags, discarded containers from hypodermics, a pair of scissors, and her own red sneakers with white laces. It wasn't apparent at first what had happened, but I was to learn in the next half hour that Indiana had taken forty-five sleeping pills, slit her wrists, and turned on the gas in the kitchen oven. It would be hard, the coroner said, to establish the true cause of death.

I got up in the middle of the night and started to prowl.

What are you looking for, Grace? I liked to talk to myself.

Nothing. I'm looking for IT.

Define IT.

The Answer. To all my questions.

You're old enough to know there's no Answer.

I was nineteen, and I did, too, think there was an Answer. I went out into the hall and down the stairs with the carved railing, pausing on the landing to look at the room Sybil sometimes used. Tonight Sybil had gone out to the diggings to sleep in her car; the back seat had been made into a bed; Sybil opened the door and filed herself into the hot plush and quilt arrangement like a letter sliding into its envelope.

The Dowells were rich and crazy and lived in French Ford because they once had ideas about an American Western Utopia. My father was a third-generation French Ford Dowell.

Down in the kitchen I leaned my head against the white-painted kitchen cabinet and cried. The crying helped some. Maybe crying was The Answer. Indiana's husband Phil had cried yesterday when they led him into his kitchen, the floor awash with Kleenex, pulmotor condensation, blood; Indy on her side with her blonde hair smeared. "There, guy, there," my father had said. Daddy was the local doctor and the Placer County Medical Administrator. He patted Phil on the arm. "Hey, now. Just to take off some of the awful edge, huh? Roll up your sleeve; here now, just a jab."

And Phil had sagged against Daddy and finally sat down on the floor and sobbed and rocked, his knees up and ankles crossed, arms locked tight around them. Phil had freckles and was an insurance agent who played golf, but he didn't look funny sitting on the floor that way.

Sybil stared at Indiana's smeared hair and put a shaking bird claw on my shoulder and said, "Satan's jewel crown."

"*What?*"

"Don't you remember? It turned to a band of red-hot iron and ate into her forehead."

Thinking about this, I stood with my own forehead against the kitchen cabinet and pressed hard, so the ridges would bite in.

After we had left Indiana's house I called Steve; he worked in a congressman's San Francisco office. It took a while to get through to him; there was a secretary and background noise and a long wait, and finally there was Steve, who said, "Hello, hello; why, Grace, Grazia, *petchild,* how *good* to hear from you." And then, when I gave him my news, he became perfectly silent. Static crackled and the French Ford cicadas outside the window

9

thrummed and squawked. Finally he sighed and said, "Well."

"Aren't you upset?" I asked, and he said, "Yes, Grace, I'm upset," the way you would speak to a child, and then he asked me when the funeral was and said he would be up for it, and after that he hung up.

I leaned against the kitchen cabinet a while longer and then decided to go up the hill to see Evva Carter. Evva was my best friend; she was also one of the town's telephone operators; tonight she would be in the phone company's Quonset hut reading her nursing textbook and punching at her circuit board.

I thought as I climbed the hill about how Evva and I had been the only girls in our third-grade class who said we wanted to go to college, and how neither of us had done it, Evva because she was too poor and I because I was waiting for Steve.

The only boy in the class who had wanted to go to college was named Duke McCracken, and he had run away from home three weeks after they asked us about college. Evva and I still talked about him, about what you did when you ran away from home and how you stayed missing.

The phone company's Quonset hut was halfway up the hill that led out of town, across the railroad tracks, on the edge of the grove of pine trees. As I climbed the hill I could see the Quonset hut's lighted window; it seemed to be shuttling back and forth among the trees, although I was the one who was moving, not it. Inside the window there was an occasional shape, maybe Evva's. Dogs sighed and grumbled in the dark houses, crickets chorused, pine tree smell rose in gusts; it had been unusually hot today.

I scratched at the Quonset hut screen door and Evva looked up from her *First Year Nursing Manual.* "Hi. I thought you'd come."

She let me in. "You've been crying."

I told her yes and sat down on the floor with my back to the ridged tin wall, and Evva went to dig in her locker for a half-empty bottle of vodka and two melamine cups. She said, "You can have it straight or you can have it straight," and I said, "Well, in that case make mine straight," and neither of us laughed. Evva sat hunched sideways in her swivel chair holding a pink plastic cup and I sat on the floor with a green plastic one.

"I guess Indy didn't trust us," I said.

"Don't say that. Maybe it came on suddenly."

After a while I said, "If she had talked to us first, . . . why didn't she tell us she was feeling bad?" and Evva said, "You don't know; you don't know."

Both of us were crying. I looked at Evva's smeared tan face and said, "Ev, I really like you; you really help me; I'm glad I didn't go away to college; what good would that have done?" and Evva said, "You might have learned something, ninny."

This sounds critical, but it didn't come across that way. The basis of our relationship was that Evva was sensible and hauled me back when I started to drift off into space. She had wanted me to go to college; mostly she had wanted it because it would have taken me away from Steve. Evva had never liked Steve, not in all the years she had known him.

Steve was my first cousin and Indiana was my second cousin.

"I've been in love with you since I was three," I told Steve the night he proposed to me.

He laughed and picked me up. I am tall, but Steve, built along the same lines as I, was both tall and sinewy. He held me up in the air, his nose at my waist; I looked down at his white-blond hair. He began to kiss me systematically, below the belt line, beginning with one pelvic bone and aiming toward the other.

"Hey, God, stop!"

He kissed the middle of my belly. I was wearing a cotton voile dress, and the kiss went through the voile. Then he put me down. "I don't remember you when you were three."

I brushed down the front of my dress. It was nine o'clock at night; we were on Main Street. There was a full moon. The white moonlight threw the jagged outline of the false-fronted Young Utopia Hall across the street surface in a black shadow. Young Utopia was a remnant of the days when the four original Dowells had come to French Ford with their railroad money and tried to found the perfect Socialist community.

Steve led me across the street to the Young Utopia porch, where we sat on the splintered steps. Moonlight squeezed through a crack between the Hall and the General Store and gilded the top of his head. He said, "If you loved me when you were three you didn't tell me."

"Why did *you* like *me?*"

He leaned back on one arm and fooled with my hair. He liked to touch me, especially my hair; he also liked to sit back and watch me after I had asked him a question.

Sometimes I thought he was playing "Mirror, mirror on the wall." Of all the Dowells, he and I were the most physically alike.

"Answer me," I said, "or I marry Mr. Griffin." Mr. Griffin was the drunk who lived across the street.

"He hasn't asked you."

"Come on. Tell me. When I was three."

"I honestly didn't know you were alive when you were three."

He let go of my hair, arched back up Young Utopia's silvered wooden steps, and flexed first one white muscled arm and then the other. "God, I'm tired. Guess what? I thought maybe you wouldn't accept me."

I returned to thinking about my romance with Steve when I was three.

Nothing can really be interesting about a three-year-old child, I decided. All the impetus has to come from the adult, no matter what Steve now claimed. I picked up various memories and settled on one about an electric train. I had been a spoiled child, with every toy imaginable, including a train set that covered the bedroom floor. You could have said that Steve played with the train because he hadn't outgrown his own childhood. But the play had involved my ordering him to crouch himself into a mountain for the trains to go around. It's hard to be sure with such early memories, but I thought I saw the scene clearly: Steve was curled, crouched on hands and knees, while I pulled switches; I was fond of accidents.

In this memory it was snowing outside; fat white flakes circled past the high windows.

"I don't think I noticed you until you were fifteen." Steve still lay slanted up the steps, arms above his head.

"You're scared of having someone think you're nice."

"Me? Scared? . . . Oh, I guess so; oh, maybe." He

stretched again, levered himself off the steps, and dusted the seat of his pants. "Good God, why should anybody think that?"

As we walked down the street he began to lecture in an excited way about the Communist Party. He was attracted, he said, to their intellectuality, their idealism, their commitment. The hell with these investigations of Communism that were popping up all over the place. Commitment and idealism were rare qualities these days. He himself didn't have them.

It was 1950, and it was risky to be talking this way, but Steve liked risk; he always had.

That was the beginning of Steve's letters to me. Like everything else about him, they were variable.

Dearest Grace:

I hope you didn't think I was being sharp, or short, or flip, or clever or more than usually conceited. That's a mask I put on. It doesn't work. Forgive.

My dear Grace, for all involved self-loathings, for introspections, intrasusceptions, denials of brightness, for flotsams washed up on beaches, forgive me in advance.

Today I had an envelope full of Constituent Queries. (English translation, Grazia, Constituent Queries are questions from voters.) And I asked Sue to put the Constituent Queries in alphabetical order. And when Sue had done that I asked her to put each voter's name on an index card. And when Sue had done that I took the cards and made marks on them. And then I told Monica Wong to send each voter a copy of the Congressman's electricity speech.

And then I went home and then I went to bed.
A collidge education is a loathsome thing, God wot.
In the original pome "rose plot" rhymes with "God
wot." But I yearn for the perfect double rhyme. Nose blot?
Toes rot?

I love you in 3/4 time

Steve worked in the San Francisco office of Congressman Jerry Shaughnessey. The office seemed to be primarily
a social work center for the Congressional District.

Darling Grace:
I am suffering from Weltschmertz, *which means world-*
sickness, which means that when I go to look at our beau-
tiful orange bridge I have trouble remembering what it is
that I am seeing.

I hope you do not keep a journal, darling Grace; people
who keep journals examine their psyches far more closely
than they should.

Aloha. The bay today was pale aluminum and the sky
was dark aluminum and I stood on an asphalt playground
wearing a gray windbreaker and yelling through a red
megaphone; the megaphone was the only spot of color on
the scene; I wanted to paint that picture except that paint-
ing pictures is the single only talent I do not have.

Love, and love

When I asked Steve if it was Indiana's diary he was
thinking of when he mentioned journals, he said he hadn't
known Indiana kept a diary.

Dear Grazia:
Here are some flowers. I picked them from some rocks
that were hanging over a cliff that I then crawled down

15

with a girl that I then was unfaithful to you with. Divorce me.

P.S. She has long red hair.

(A postcard)
Dear Grace:
Disregard last letter.

Dear Grace:
I am tormenting myself rather than you.
I made it up
in a moment of purest
loneliness, terror

Dear Grace:
Today I am going through the file in search of Dead Names. Dead Names are constituents who have moved, or perhaps even died.

I am also reading Marx's CAPITAL for the 4th time and asking myself if it still makes sense and am unsure whether yes or no. But I love him for his long Germanic sentences and his massive Teutonic intellect and the relentlessness and absolute logic of that step-by-step inevitable reasoning so that eventually he piles brick on brick into a monstrous wonderful monument to a wonderful and terrible cause.

Love always, always love,
S.

(A postcard showing a picture of The Delta Hotel, Stockton, Calif.)

Dear Grace:
X marks my room.
Wish you were here.

Love, S.

3

I was up at six on the day of Indiana's funeral; I stood at the open window of my room and stared out at a town emerging from its background of blue impressionist particles. A few pale landmarks collected light into themselves: the yellow Southern Pacific Founders' House, the front of the school, the tower of the church where Indiana's funeral would be held.

I had found a black dress for myself in Mother's cedar closet. Most of my mother's clothes had been preserved, for eighteen years now, in this cedar-lined partitioned closet. I chose another dress for Sybil. Sybil didn't like to accept hand-me-downs—she liked to steal, but apparently she thought of stealing things as control, accepting them as being out of control. She had examined this dress carefully, peered at the seams, held the material up to the light, and finally, maybe because of the I. Magnin label, agreed: "Well. It *is* a well-constructed garment."

The sleeves of Sybil's dress were different from the sleeves that were being worn now, but the length was all right. My own dress was a straight sheath and seemed strange in this year of full skirts; I had picked it because it was sleeveless. I tried to imagine my mother wearing it, with high-heeled shoes and a close-fitting sequinned hat. The dress hung now on a padded hanger, suspended from the molding that marked the top of my wallpaper.

"What a shame," Sybil said as I came downstairs, "I wanted to make breakfast for the family, and now *everybody* is in the kitchen, everybody."

She had spent the night in her room off the landing, to be on hand for the funeral. By *everybody* she meant Mrs. Farmer, our housekeeper, who cooked dinner for us six nights a week. Mrs. Farmer had come over this morning; she was worried about us.

Sybil was fixing eggs, Mrs. Farmer told me. Sybil would do one of her egg recipes. "Sharing your cooking is a way of knowing the truth." Mrs. Farmer was a Christian Scientist.

"It's a way of giving people breakfast." Sybil sounded jumpy. I asked her which egg recipe she was planning. Sybil had fourteen ways of cooking hard-boiled eggs. I didn't want hard-boiled eggs this morning.

"It is to be Eggs Benedict," Mrs. Farmer said. "Eggs Benedict are comforting; I am preparing the egg poacher and Lloyd McCracken will bring the eggs."

Mrs. Farmer was wearing a black rayon dress but it had a white pique collar with ducks embroidered along its border and she didn't look funereal, just professional and motherly. The kitchen was nice this morning, with the bright blue French Ford light pouring through the high windows; the light hit the top of Sybil's white head and the shoulders of her orange Chinese robe. This scene, also, did not look funereal.

"Is it always like this," I asked, "part of you says everything is different and part says it's just the same?"

"Indiana is not different; she is passed on," Mrs. Farmer said. "Death shall have no dominion."

Sybil said, "Yes, it's always the same; you are sad and God is glad."

Sybil looked fiercely at Mrs. Farmer. I was relieved when there was a clatter at the screen door.

Lloyd McCracken was a brother of Duke McCracken, the one who had run away from home when he was nine. Lloyd leaned against our porch wall, one shoulder higher than the other, and held the eggs, in a cardboard box, level out in front of him. He straightened as I came up. "I'm sorry to hear about your trouble; these here are a present." He extended the box, his narrow wary McCracken face waiting to be rejected.

The McCrackens were the largest French Ford family except for the Dowells; there was a network of cousins and uncles and there were three of these McCracken boys besides the missing Duke. They were good at riding motorcycles and at shooting holes in beer cans.

I held the screen door ajar. "Come on in, Lloyd; Sybil is fixing eggs; why don't you stay for breakfast?"

I think it was Sybil's statement about God being glad that made me do this. Sybil looked exhausted; now I had to worry about her, too. A generous gesture was a counteraction to Sybil's thinking God was glad.

Lloyd told Sybil that her Eggs Benedict were real cool. I expected her to argue with him about this phrase, but she seemed to understand right away. My father joined us as the eggs were being put on the table. Daddy looked tired; his pale Dowell face was all lines and hollows, but he perked up when he saw Lloyd. "Hey, Lloyd, hey, guy, what say?" Daddy called me Babe; he addressed other men as "hey." "Hey," he said to Lloyd, and made a motion as if he were going to punch him on the arm. Lloyd laughed and sparred, and Daddy laughed, too. My father was supposed to be the town intellectual. I stared at him and thought, Maybe it's fun not being the intellectual for a while. I also asked myself, as Daddy sparred with Lloyd, if he ought to be doing that. My father had had several heart attacks; I wasn't supposed to know about them.

"You are behaving like children," Sybil told them.

Daddy talked to Lloyd about tattoos, and about the best speed for riding a motorcycle across Utah. We had a pleasant breakfast.

At ten-thirty the church bells started tolling, and Sybil, Mrs. Farmer, Daddy, and I began our walk down the hill. I held a white beaded pocketbook and wore white mesh gloves. Evva had made me a black hat. Evva was clever with her hands.

"That young man has no sense of other people's needs," Sybil said. She was talking about Steve.

"Steve's not going to be late." My father liked Steve, who was the other town intellectual. "Steve's okay about stuff like this."

"I know I don't come first," Sybil said. "I understand that perfectly. What are you staring at?"

"You." Sybil looked tired, just as we all did, but she looked worse. There was a dusting of gray across her cheekbones, as if she had found gray, instead of pink, face powder somewhere. She negotiated the downhill walk suspiciously, afraid of being grabbed by gravity. When I took her arm she resisted at first and then rested on me.

I supported her and scanned the road for rocks, and watched, out of the corner of my eye, the slope of the opposite hill where Steve would come down from the highway. He drove a red Cord convertible; after he had cleared the slope he would gun his motor to make an echo.

The day was hot; the church bell bonged: key of C, key of C. I tried to think of something happy. On V-E Day we had come to this church to rejoice; it was an impromptu service; bells rang; people brought armloads of laurel, manzanita, pine cones. We held hands and sang "The Battle Hymn of the Republic," and smiled at each other and at our stained glass window, where a strawberry-blond Jesus ministered to men in boots and miners' helmets. My grandparents had given the window to the church; as Socialists they had believed in Topical Art.

I held the hymnal for Sybil and absorbed neutral impressions: today's hymn ("I Bind Unto Myself"), Sybil's rhinestone pin, Evva's crisp brown curls. In the hymn rack in front of us was more Dowell Socialism: a book from the parish library: *Communal Life in the Catacombs*. After a while I heard Steve's car cough; he hadn't gunned the motor today, in deference to Indiana. And finally Mrs. Farmer squeezed over to make a space for him, and he fitted in beside me and put a hand across the small of my back.

Reverend Lloyd's voice moved into the Twenty-third Psalm. Sybil tilted unsteadily. Ahead, in the center of the aisle, in front of the altar, was Indiana's purple casket with a cloth over it. The church was full; everybody in French Ford had come to Indiana's funeral.

In the French Ford Cemetery, on a hill overlooking the south end of town, the bend in Main Street, the back of the Methodist Church, Steve and I stood beside Indiana's freshly filled grave. The other mourners had already gone down the hill to the reception at Phil's mother's house. "Aren't you coming? The car will drive us down," my father had suggested, and "You *should* come. Now," Sybil had ordered, but Steve, with a hand on my shoulder, had said, "We'll just wait here a minute, Auntie Sybil," looking directly into her eyes, smiling his best slightly crooked smile, making it somehow apparent that remaining behind would be of help to *me*.

The chopped earth of Indiana's grave was covered with a mat of imitation grass and surrounded with piles of pink gladioli, purple and yellow chrysanthemums, white lilies. "What you don't understand," Steve said, "is that that depression—that feeling Indiana had—it comes and grabs you from behind, holds you the way a cop holds a rioter— you can't understand that, you're too normal, Grazia, to know about it."

Steve called me Grazia or Carissima only sometimes. I thought it was when he wanted to put distance between us.

"I understand, all right."

But Steve went right on talking; he seemed not to have heard me. "It's like being captured by the Snow Queen. Do you remember about the Snow Queen, Grazia? Remember what she did to people?"

"She turned Little Kay's heart into an ice splinter."

He looked down at me. Something in the light green eyes

seemed to be fear. "Why, yes. She did do that, didn't she, hollowed out his insides . . ."

"No," I corrected. "It happened from inside *him*. Because he wanted to be frozen."

"Ah." He curled and uncurled a wisp of my hair, one of those insubstantial ones at the back of the neck. "Do you think I'm arrogant, Grace? An arrogant bastard?"

"No."

He ran his open hand down my backbone. Mother's black dress was silk, and had stuck to me in the heat. "How long will that reception last?"

When I didn't answer he turned, hand still on my back, toward the town. It lay below us, hazy with early afternoon heat, ripples of mirage rising from the asphalt sections of Main Street and from the corrugated tin roofs.

I used to have a fantasy about French Ford being a paperweight, one of those elegantly detailed scenes in a glass bubble; you shake it and particles of snow or glitter rise up to enhance the landscape.

"What do you say?" Steve asked. "Shall we put on a display for the natives? Sex in the graveyard? On the graves of our ancestors? That's what everybody expects of us, isn't it?"

"No."

"What would Indiana expect?"

"Steve, stop it."

"Shall I tell you about me and Indiana?"

"No."

He stared around us, at the monuments with their bent, Greek-robed figures, at Indiana's electric-green artificial grass. "Do you think about where you and I will be? For *our* eternal rest?"

"They're waiting for us."

Steve's arm quivered slightly, as if a galvanic current ran through it. "They expect it. They expect us . . . to misbehave . . ." He tugged me. "It's over here, Where we'll be." I let him pull me past Indiana's artificial blanket, her mound of purple and yellow flowers. "Would she have liked those colors?" he asked.

"Please. Let's leave."

"I love you. And here is where we'll be buried." He took off his jacket and tossed it onto the mat of juniper and laurel. The undergrowth released a sharp smell. Insects hummed angrily. "Grandparents on one side." He patted a stone angel. "Aunts on the other. Indiana at our feet."

He turned to me, positioned his hands on my shoulders, inclined his head, and kissed me, first with his mouth closed, then with it open. I felt the lines of his body through his thin cotton shirt: the hard bite of his rib cage, the cavity below that, the declivity where the belly went in, the angle of the belt buckle, finally the swelling of his erection. He pulled his head back and looked down at me.

He had lowered his eyelashes over his light eyes; it was hard to read his expression. "Grace," he said, "don't ever think people don't expect something of you. They expect the worst."

He moved his hand down my back, let it linger at my waist, brought it around my body, across the bottom of my abdomen. I said, "Don't."

He began to take off his clothes, deliberately, not very fast: shirt, tie: he stripped these off and threw them on his jacket. He wasn't wearing an undershirt. He sat down on the pile of clothing, pulled off shoes, socks, squeezed out of his pants. For a minute then he sat forward, his arms

24

around his knees. The sun gilded his silver body hair. Finally he stood and faced me; he was completely naked.

We didn't touch. The metallic odor of my damp black dress surrounded me; around him was a haze of sunmotes, bronze, silver. I thought: *He's not too thin. I thought he would be too thin.* After a while Steve pushed me down onto the pile of clothing.

The crickets thrummed, the telephone wires buzzed; far off in the distance, perhaps as far away as Colfax, a train sounded. He lay on top of me, his finger outlining a nipple. He pulled up my dress. I said, "Steve."

"Do you love me?"

"Yes."

"Do you really love me?"

"Yes." All the blood in my body was concentrated in the places where he pushed against me.

"Say it. You love me."

"I love you. I love you."

He sighed, moved his head into the crook of my neck, and bit. His hair scraped the bitten place. "You don't."

"Steve."

He had begun to lose his erection. "You don't love me."

"I do."

"And that's how the story ends."

The train called three times. It was getting closer. "What story? What's wrong?"

"Nothing. All stories. That's how they end." He got up, deliberately, and stared down, eyelids half closed over light eyes. "Let's pull ourselves together. They're waiting for us."

Before we left he grabbed me by the shoulders. "Grace," he said. "Grace, help me."

4

"You are wasting your entire life," Evva Carter had told me the year we were both thirteen.

We were sitting in a corner of the Colfax High School playground eating our lunch. Evva's lunch was a bologna, lettuce, and mayonnaise sandwich on Wonder Bread; mine was pork pâté on rye. My father had made the pâté; because of the war, he had had to make it with ground-up Spam. Daddy was an excellent gourmet cook. I picked up a corner of the rye bread and surveyed the pebbled pâté texture, flecked with scraps of basil, and thought that the difference between Evva's and my lunches reflected the difference between our lives. "I'm not," I told her.

"He's old enough to be your . . ." Evva paused. "Nothing will ever happen to you as long as you're waiting for him." She meant Steve.

"*You* are in love with Lloyd McCracken."

A basketball game was in progress in the far corner of the playground. The boys wore gray shorts; the brilliant sunlight made all their figures the same bleached color.

The noise of the game reached us as muffled thunks and thuds.

"Lloyd McCracken is okay," Evva said, her voice too high. "I'm not in love with him."

Evva had talked to me about Lloyd during one of the periods when she was not really not in love with him. She had said that she liked to watch Lloyd ride his motorcycle, especially standing up. She liked to sit behind him on the cycle and feel the back of his rib cage and the seam of his leather jacket. I had nodded when she talked this way. It was all pretty clear and straightforward and not a mystery like the question of what on earth I might be wanting from Steve. I thought of Steve's light-green staccato eyes and shivered.

The phrase "staccato eyes" was one I had stolen from Scott Fitzgerald, but I often used it when I thought about Steve. Fitzgerald was Steve's favorite writer. Steve had discovered Fitzgerald the winter before that one, when I was twelve, and had immediately shared him with me and Daddy; he had read the "staccato eyes" story aloud to us in our living room. Steve had a trained tenor voice and read marvelously. But when my father, seated in his armchair, hands arranged into a tent, said, "Tell me, Steve, what is it you like especially?" Steve wouldn't say.

"All of us neurotics stick together, Blake."

"Listen, I like it, too. I'm crazy about it. But what, exactly?"

"He's a wonderful writer. A specific, precise writer."

"So's Hemingway."

"There are fewer animals in Fitzgerald. More people."

"Come on, now."

Steve turned a page. The short story was set in midsummer, in the northern Midwest; we sat in our green living room, in November French Ford. The brass fire dogs and the brass fire screen had been polished that morning by Mrs. Farmer. Orange fire-glow moved back and forth on the smooth surfaces and reflected itself up into Steve's face. At twenty-two, Steve's face was already dented and drawn, like the one I imagined Scott Fitzgerald himself having. Steve was in uniform, a dark blue naval lieutenant's one. He had been posted to Treasure Island in San Francisco Bay, doing something with codes and ciphers.

"Death and madness," he said pleasantly, as if offering a recipe. "That's what's special about Fitzgerald."

"*This* story is about visions," I objected.

"It's about *not* having them." Steve went back to reading aloud, using his trained voice so well that I forgot I was being read to, and moved into the country of the story. But a few minutes later he put the book facedown on the floor and said he had a headache. "I think maybe this one is about betrayal, Grace." He rubbed his forehead with his hand. "Don't you think so?"

I didn't answer. I was old enough to know that adults sometimes asked questions to which they didn't really want answers.

"Well, good luck," I said to Evva about Lloyd. "I mean, I hope it all sifts out." I thought about Lloyd's narrow face and was not intrigued. But I could certainly understand about the motorcycle.

When I got home I asked my father how long he had been in love with my mother when he married her.

He looked up from his book. "Hey, Babe. I mean. That's a solemn question. You got the solemnities or something?"

Daddy's book was about bookbinding: how to prepare the leather for the book's cover, how to stipple the page edges. My father was interested in everything: sociology, bird-watching, journalism, you name it. I dropped my school binder on the overstuffed hassock. "I need to know."

Daddy shifted. "Babe, I think it was . . . maybe six months . . ." He squinted past me. "Why, honey? Historical research?"

"Not especially."

"So why?"

"Why not?"

I picked up my school binder and went upstairs, where I slammed myself down onto the window seat and stared out at the town. The same town, as usual: tin roofs, white and yellow houses. I was right to be in love with Steve. Steve was the only person in the world who took me seriously.

After a while I heard Daddy in the hall. When I turned around he was stooped forward in the door, staring at me, his head jutting out. "Listen, Babe."

"Yes, Father." I enjoyed responding to Babe with Father.

"Baby, I've been thinking. When the war is over . . ." (*When this cruel war is over*, that was a song that they played over and over on the Midas truck-stop jukebox.)

Daddy was talking. ". . . send you away to school, or college, or just on a trip . . . so you'll have something different . . . I'm sorry, Babe." Daddy brushed at his fading hair; a hunk of it hung down across his forehead.

I said, "Thank you, Daddy," and, after a minute, "Thank you, really," and stared at him, and noticed his

29

pop-eyes, and wondered if they were a symptom of heart trouble.

Nothing ever stayed the way you thought it was when you had it figured out.

The next afternoon I took the school bus home and walked from the bus stop to Indiana's house.

Indiana had been married to Phil for just two months and was still getting wedding presents. It was exciting to come into her living room and push aside the paper labels and package wrappings, and admire the enamelled steel bowls, the silver soup ladles, the blown glass vases.

I am not sure what made me circle the house before knocking on the front door screen that jangled when you touched it. Perhaps I wanted to feel from all sides the house of a newly married couple. As I crossed the back lawn and circled the pink terra-cotta birdbath I had a clear view into Indiana's newly decorated kitchen with the white cupboards and red tiled floor. The tiled floor, which Indiana was still houseproud enough to scrub every day, was not empty. Two people were lying together in the middle of it. Indiana and Steve were both clothed, but they were rumpled and tightly entangled; Steve, on his back, seemed to be staring up at the ceiling; Indiana, half on her side, lay on top of him, her head wedged in the crook of his neck.

Neither of them moved as I went by, although it seemed to me that I must have made a perceptible change in the shapes of the garden.

5

Sybil had been acting strangely ever since Indiana's death. "Grace, dear," Mrs. Farmer said, "I don't like to mention this because I don't like to court error."

With Sybil you didn't need to wonder if something was the matter; you knew. She was stealing more flagrantly: large things, awkward things, things that were alive, like the postmistress's calico cat. The cat had jumped out of Sybil's arms and run off down Main Street as soon as she let go of it, so technically she hadn't stolen it. But still she had marched down Main Street out of the Post Office with it, announcing, "This is my cat. Its name is Aurelia." Sybil talked to herself in a language that sounded like French but that I was pretty sure wasn't; one of her eyes didn't focus; it rolled over and watched a corner of the sky. Mrs. Farmer was right; she needed help.

I walked out to the diggings thinking about Sybil and the ways she made you want to help her. It had something to do with her attempts to straighten her curved back, and with her poetic vocabulary.

When I got to the Buick I found her sitting in one of her lawn chairs, wedged up against the side of the car to catch the shade. She was knitting.

"Would you like to come stay with us for a week?" I asked.

The knitting was white and was taking forever. I suspected Sybil of picking it apart at night, like Penelope. She clicked for a while. "Why?"

I improvised. "Daddy's having a party. He needs your help."

"In that case," she agreed. We went back to the Buick and packed some clothes in a laundry bag. Sybil said I was supposed to carry this on my head, but I chose instead to hold it in front of me, wedged on my belt buckle.

"All right, but not great," was Mrs. Farmer's verdict, after a dinner that had gone well except for a misunderstanding about the pepper. After dinner Sybil went up to bed early, complimenting me on the beauty of the white bedspread. When I asked if there was anything she needed she said, "Good heavens, child. *I* should be asking *you* that," and held up her arms to be kissed.

But the next morning she woke me at six by scratching on the outside walls of the house. The noise was a penetrating one that sawed through my sleep and wouldn't be accommodated by dreams about motorboats or air raid warnings. I went outside, and there was Sybil, dressed in a plaid nightgown and a pink feather boa, chiseling at the shingles with a screwdriver. "I am looking for a message from that poor child."

"What poor child?"

"Indiana." She had got the screwdriver under a shingle

and was prying vigorously. It made a destructive noise. "She left a message."

"Indiana didn't leave a message, Aunt Sybil. You saw." I didn't want to be too specific about the scene in Indiana's kitchen.

"Oh, yes. Indiana had a diary. It was bound in Japanese block print and had a blue back. Your father will tell you, I am psychic." She dropped her screwdriver and began tugging at things with her bare fingers.

"Aunt Sybil, for God's sake, quit pulling the house apart."

"In a dark and secret place."

"Well, the front of our house isn't dark and secret. It's painted white."

She stared at me and said, "Yes, yes, that's true," and let a piece of siding snap back into place. Then she pushed past me into the front door, the feather boa trailing pinkly behind. It was a skinny boa and was shedding fronds of feather. It had been my mother's; I wondered if Mother had bought it seriously or as a joke. There was a lot about my mother I didn't know.

An hour later Sybil could not be found, and even though I didn't think she had gone home, I went out to the diggings, where there was nothing of her except her baking-hot car. Then I borrowed Daddy's Jeep and drove to Midas. The University of California's experimental mine, where Sybil had taken me when I was two, was in Midas.

The university had closed Diaspora Mine shortly after Sybil kidnapped me; they had built a cement wall across the entrance. But everyone in Placer County knew that

33

there was another way in, behind the switchman's shed at Midas crossing.

I pulled Daddy's Jeep up beside the yellow switchman's storage shed, got out our heavy-duty battery-powered lantern, and began to poke around in the bushes, looking for the right manzanita plant. I had not been here for six years.

"Your whole life is spent with people older than you," Steve had told me. You're right Steve, I thought. Crawling down holes looking for them. Rescuing, saving. "The only trouble with you," Evva said, "is you think you're God."

"All the Dowells think they're God."

"Shut up about the Dowells."

Sybil had marked her trail well. Bent bushes, kicked-up dirt, even a scrap of herself, or rather of my mother, a shred of pink marabou feather. I bent double and squeezed backwards into the low, grainy, powdery hole. Tight, scary. I was bigger now than I had been at thirteen.

I wasn't going to worry about the tunnel falling in on me. It had been here for ninety years, hadn't it?

The Dowells didn't believe in God; they believed in the basic goodness of people, which formed a universal spirit around them like a warm fog around a streetlight.

I decided not to call Sybil's name, because I had a mental picture of her standing on the edge of the elevator shaft, hearing the name and saying, "*Stop* bothering me," or "A dark and secret place," and then jumping, hair flying out behind her.

Diaspora was a peculiar name for a mine. Did the original Dowells think they were the exiled Jewish people?

The mine had been a true working one before the university took it over. It had a railroad with one car that scooted on a single rail, a conveyor belt for buckets, several passageways, and an empty elevator shaft. The air inside the mine was dry and even-temperatured; part of the soil was dry and red, like the soil of French Ford, another part was dry and white, like that around the Quarry Pit; the whole with a clean, sandy underground smell.

I was now at the main corridor; here was the railroad car, parked cockeyed, looking dusty and expensive; the university had bought a new car for its students and had painted it red with gold trim, like a Victorian toy. It was loaded with neat dusty rocks.

Myths, monsters, and legends lived in Diaspora. There was a colony of eyeless white bears, a mad hermit who saved Pepsi-Cola bottles, a mad hermit with a hoard of gold. I wasn't afraid of the dark; the dark was a place to think in. Close the door, the light is wrecking my thoughts.

Overhead were stands where carbide lanterns had once sat. People had stolen the lanterns, brass ones with curlicues. I squeezed by the railroad car, slipping on the powdery slope. Walking sideways was the best way to go, with my butt lodged against the wall of the tunnel. How had Sybil managed? "Your aunt is simply marvelous; I surely hope I'm as full of ideas and energy at her age."

Here was the place where Indiana had walked on the railroad ties. Evva and I had been thrilled when she came into the mine with us that summer. Why had she wanted to do anything with *us?* Indiana was seventeen then and we were only thirteen: maybe she was bored, maybe she was simply nice. "This place scares me," she had said, "not the tightness of it, but all those miles and miles of nothing, spread out, interleaved, veins in somebody's body." She had the same kind of mind Sybil did, but less dotty; she extended her hands under our flashlight beam to demonstrate about the veins. When we got to the iron railroad ties she had put her arm around my waist; her hair touched my cheek. That was flattering, and she smelled good. "Listen to our footsteps," she said, "bang bang; the iron maidens."

The wall to the right of me spelled out, in white pebbles stuck into dirt, "Kilroy was here." I went into the first side tunnel. It was level-floored, and I could stand straight in it. It held the remains of a picnic: paper plates, napkins, the dried twisted peel of some fruit. The second corridor had an orange-crate desk with a sign on it: *Susan Freeman, we hate you.* For the last part of the corridor I balanced on the center rail, thinking that anything you do you get good at after a while, and you are always learning to do things that you never have a chance to practice again.

The three remaining passages had junk in them, mostly from children's secret societies. And now there was nothing left except the elevator shaft, which I had been circling around.

It was an empty shaft that had once held a freight elevator. It went down the center of the mine. There were narrow places off it where digging had started, and you used to be able to lie in these passages and dig, and send the results up on a bucket.

I turned off the main circular driveway that held the railroad car and headed for the elevator shaft. The ground sloped slightly; in a plan, the shape of the mine would have looked like a shallow Chinese workman's hat, upside down.

I made speeches to Sybil in my head: Aunt Sybil, you are the limit. Sybil, what are you trying to do?

A skeletal framework, irrational in my lantern beam, was the sign that I had reached the elevator shaft. This framework surrounded the hole that used to contain the elevator machinery. I crawled under the framework and shone my light down.

"Sybil." My beam at first wouldn't penetrate. Then, finally, I had it: a heap of clothes like a piled set of quilts or blankets, a curlicue of pink marabou across the top.

"Sybil."

No answer.

"Darling, please answer me."

Nothing.

"Sybil, please." I stretched farther into the opening and moved the light. Maybe I saw a tremor in the clothing. "You can have my amethyst pin."

A sigh. After a minute an arm, pale blue in the lantern beam, raised out of the clothes, elbow foremost. "I didn't do it."

"I knew you wouldn't."

"I thought about it. And then I didn't. But I contemplated it."

"That's okay."

"Do you think, Grace, contemplating will take the place of action?"

"Yes, I think so." It was odd, speaking down into the pit at a pile of plaid flannel and pink feathers and the upraised elbow. Sybil's face was hiding somewhere inside. "Shall I come down and get you?"

"Maybe."

I hung the lantern around my neck and turned around and started to climb down the inside of the frame. It was made of flat steel struts, crossed and bolted. They were uncomfortably spaced for climbing.

When I got to the bottom I squatted and Sybil turned over. "It was rather nice," she said. She pushed her face

37

out from under the pink fur. "I closed my eyes and pretended I was dead."

"How was that?"

"Restful. Non-objective. I lay here and thought about that word: *non-objective.*"

I said, "It's time we went back up. Sit up now."

"You sound like a ward attendant."

"Well, we have to do it."

She flopped around a bit, like a bug on its back. "I feel weak."

I grabbed a wrist. "Here we go."

Maybe it was my tone of voice that decided her. "I can't."

"You haven't broken anything?"

"No."

I kept hold of her wrist. She looked at my hand. "That's all there is to it, Grace. I can't. I'll have to be carried."

I stopped squatting and sat down. There was no way I could carry Sybil up the elevator frame. "Are you dizzy?"

"No."

"Does your head hurt? Stomach ache?"

"Goodness, no." Her voice rose with what sounded like pleasure. "I simply can't."

"Oh," I said. "Okay." I arranged myself more comfortably, with my back against the frame. How long would Daddy's lantern battery last?

"You can turn the light off if you want to," Sybil said.

I snapped it off.

"Tell me how you guessed I was here."

"Sybil, I won't talk to you until you start climbing out of here."

In a while she said, "It's not on purpose. It's a weakness, like a moral weakness."

I snapped the light back on. After all, Sybil had a flash-light, which she had not been using. We had two lights. "Maybe you'll feel better soon."

"Maybe."

Sybil began to sing. First she sang the chorus of "The Battle Hymn of the Republic." Then she started on "Amazing Grace." She sang it quite well. "You were named for that song," she said, pausing between verses.

"Nonsense."

"No, really. Your father didn't know that, but I did. Your mother used to sing it; she liked the part about "I, at last, am free.""

"What did she want to be free of?"

"She didn't know."

The more I heard about my mother the sadder I felt for her.

Sybil began the second verse of "Amazing Grace," and I said, "Hush." Somewhat to my surprise she stopped sing-ing immediately. Maybe she had heard the footsteps, too.

They were an indistinct rhythm for a while, an echo in the wall, and then they got clearer, and after a while I was certain; they really were footsteps coming toward us.

A blur appeared at the top of the elevator shaft. I shone my light up, and it was a human face. Everyone looks alike lighted from below that way, so I aimed the light down. The person said, "Are you hurt?" It was a man's voice.

"I don't think so."

"What happened?"

I told him. He said, "Oh," and then, "Well, I'll come down." And a minute later a pair of brown loafers ap-proached, feeling their way along the frame.

There wasn't much room at the bottom. The new person had to stand up.

39

He aimed his flashlight beam tactfully near us but not directly at us and said, "Oh, it's Mrs. Dowell." Sybil had been married so many times that the neighborhood had given up on her last name and simply called her Dowell.

"And you," the man said, "are . . ."—I thought he was going to say "Indiana"—"Grace Dowell."

The flashlight made it hard to be sure, but this person seemed familiar. "Do I know you?"

"You used to. I'm David . . . Duke McCracken."

"Duke?" I said. "Duke Mc*Crack*en?"

He said yes in the voice people use when they have had to say something too often, and I said, "You ran away from home when you were nine," and he said, "Yes," as if he were trying to be polite, and then, before I could ask any more he said, "Come on, Mrs. Dowell, maybe I can get you out of here. We'll try a fireman's carry. I learned it at school."

Sybil liked the idea of the fireman's carry and cooperated. She let herself be draped over his shoulder with her legs limp.

There was a bit of maneuvering to get her through the framework and over the lip of the elevator shaft, but in the middle of that she said, "I can walk, really I can," and squeezed through on her own power.

After that we trudged decorously to the entrance of the tunnel, I in front holding Sybil's hand, she following behind me. It didn't take long and the only conversation was my "Thank you, Duke, a lot," and his "That's okay."

When we were outside I said, "What made you go into the mine?"

He smiled. He had a nice smile. "I saw your Jeep outside and I wondered. You left the motor running."

40

I didn't know I had left the motor running and ran toward the Jeep. "I turned it off," Duke said. "I put the keys in the glove compartment."

"Thank you."

"When I got inside the mine," he said, "I heard someone singing hymns. That seemed ominous."

He laughed, and in a minute I did too.

I examined him. I could see that he might be a Mc-Cracken; he had the same narrow face bones, but his hair was darker and he was taller and more finished looking than his brothers. He looked like a college student. "Thank you, Duke."

"My name's David." He read my expression and went on. "David's *really* my name. The District Nurse named me. My family *called* me Duke."

He and I got Sybil bundled into the passenger side of the Jeep and I said, "Are you back in French Ford now?" wondering why I hadn't heard about this; I liked to think that I knew everything that happened in French Ford.

David stared at me. "Well, no. I work in San Francisco."

After a minute he added, "I work in the same office as your cousin. Your . . . fiancé. Steve. I'm the college intern."

"I am feeling very cold," Sybil said plaintively.

There didn't seem to be much else to say, so I told David, "Thank you; thank you very much," and we stared at each other for a while before I started up the Jeep.

6

"Steve," I said, "why didn't you tell me about David Mc-
Cracken?"

Steve said, "What *about* David McCracken? Am I supposed to tell you every single gossipy thing that happens?"
A minute later he said, "His name is *Duke* McCracken,"
and after that, "He's the *college* intern, for Christ's sake."
Then he went out the screen door, slamming it successfully
in spite of its rubber-ball stopper.

Steve had been back in French Ford for three days. It
seemed ridiculous to say that I didn't know why he was
here, but it was true.

After he left I lay down on the oriental rug; it was mid-
day; I was on page 169 of *The Magic Mountain.* I liked
The Magic Mountain; its enclosed world reminded me of
French Ford.

I wasn't sure what was wrong with Steve.

He was worried about Indiana, about me, about us.

"You project too much," my father had said during one of his psychiatric phases.

Later that night I saw Steve outside the General Store. He was leaning against the storefront, holding a beer in one hand, talking to Lloyd and Argo McCracken. His dog was there, stretched out on its side in the dust; there were also three McCracken dogs, all the same shade of yellow-white; the McCrackens seemed to have produced a pure breed of dog that looked like that, yellow-white with yellow eyes and a dirty pink muzzle: thoroughbred mongrels, Daddy had called them, smiling as he invented the phrase.

With his usual investigative curiosity Daddy had brought home a book on genetics from the University of California library; he was interested in those yellow-white dogs and wanted to find out how the McCrackens made them breed so true.

Yellow-white genes, I think the book said, were dominant, at least in dogs.

Steve's dog was an Irish setter, orange-red, with orange-red eyes. She was pedigreed and had cost two hundred dollars.

I sat on our porch steps and stared down the road at Steve and the McCrackens. They made an enclosed, unapproachable male unit. I didn't want to go down and speak to them, although I had thought of calling out to Steve when he banged out of the house this morning.

Argo McCracken wore khaki army pants and leaned against the red gas pump gesturing with a beer can; Buddy McCracken squatted on the ground, his hands loosely resting on his knees. I could hear the vibrations of his voice from here, but not what he said. Steve, posed against the storefront, looked more graceful than Argo. But he was in accord with his surroundings, too. No one seeing this group of men would have thought Steve any different from the others. The dogs were clustered in the middle, not on top of each other, because it was too hot, but with parts of their bodies touching.

I didn't know why I felt love and sorrow and wanted to send them down the road to Steve.

"Quit trying so hard," I said to the blue and yellow design on the cover of *The Magic Mountain*.

The next morning when I opened the back screen door there was a branch of manzanita, bright silver, propped against the screen. It tumbled over and fell down the steps as I opened the door. Manzanita is a plant whose bark is silver during part of its year and red during another part. It's hard to find pure silver manzanitas, usually they are shedding and parti-colored, frayed, like peeling sunburn. I went down the steps and picked up the branch; it was still unscarred and bright. It had a note tied to it: *"Grace: I love you. (SIGNED) God."*

Oh, well, I wondered whether to put the spray in water or not, and finally didn't.

"We should have screwed in the graveyard." Steve sat in the front seat of his convertible. The top was down; the wind had blown his hair into a pale ruff. He stared at me somberly. I stood on the street holding a dishtowel; I had come out of the house when I saw the car. He said, "I'm driving to Reveille."

I threw the dishtowel into the purple hydrangea bush and walked around to the passenger side. Steve held the door for me. He handed me a white silk scarf with strawberries on it. "I bought it for you. This afternoon. It was to benefit the Ladies' Aid."

I ignored his remark about the graveyard. "That was loyal of you, supporting the Ladies' Aid." The wind slapped at the scarf; it was white parachute silk; by some accident the Ladies' Aid member had positioned her strawberries in interesting ways.

Steve drove with one hand and rested the other on the car door. "What have you been doing?"

Scenery went by. The climb from French Ford to Reveille was steep; the terrain changed dramatically: red clay became granite outcroppings and gravel; tall, hopeful deep green pines changed to contorted gray ones. There was nothing at Reveille once you got there; the whole point of the drive was the drop in temperature and the feeling of motion.

"I've not been doing much," I said finally. "Just leaning against the front of the General Store. Talking to the Mc-Crackens. Drinking beer. Spitting on the sidewalk."

Steve showed me his profile and smiled the vulnerable smile that pulled his mouth-corners smooth. "Shall we go down into the town?"

"Yes."

"Actually," he said, "I *was* drinking beer, but I was thinking of *you*." He made the turn off the highway. The convertible roared, and its outside exhaust pipes quivered.

Reveille was the best place in Placer County for listening to trains. The town of Reveille was five hundred feet down from the highway, along a steep graveled road, across a ford. Once it had sheltered a pleasant country hotel with wide porches and adjacent shingled cottages. Part of the hotel building was still there; it contained a store in which one could buy Coca-Cola, beer, vodka, and whiskey, and a room where my father had his weekly clinic. Four of the cottages survived under steeply shedding roofs. Splintered two-by-fours and heaps of shingles indicated where the other cottages had been; they were arranged in a semicircle around something that still made a dent in the leafy soil, a pond, maybe. The remainder of Reveille was a scattering of one-story houses, most of them painted Southern Pacific yellow.

Neither Steve nor I commented on the appearance of Reveille; we had known it all our lives.

Steve parked the car in front of the Coca-Cola store. The children from the end cottage came out on their front steps to watch us.

"There's a train in ten minutes." Steve led the way to a pile of lumber beside the railroad track and climbed on top of it. There was canvas stretched across the wood, so we didn't need to worry about splinters.

The sun had already moved behind the Reveille hills but it hadn't yet set; the sky was bright. Steve settled himself on the lumber pile. "I think I hear it." He put his arm around me.

"I like you," I said, "when you're like this."

He stared at the sunlit part of the sky. "And not other times."

"I love you. All the time."

He removed the arm. "You sound like my mother."

This wasn't a compliment. Steve's mother was a frightened lady with wire hair who spent her life complaining. "I can hear the train, too."

The railroad circled Reveille in an arc. For twenty minutes the train would travel and the air would vibrate.

"An *up* train," I said. Noises were different for up trains and for down trains.

"Hey," Steve grabbed my hand, "it sounds like Jerry Shaughnessey. Like my honored congressman."

The bass train-noises were regulating themselves now, heavily metallic. "I didn't think Jerry Shaughnessey sounded like that."

"He sounds like a big tank of wind."

"I thought you liked him."

"I do. Sure an' I do. When he stares at you with those wet Irish eyes an' says, 'Stevie. My boy. The working man's day. Is comin'.'" Steve shifted, the lumber pile creaked. He put his arm around his shins and rested his chin on his knees.

"You told me he was the real thing. You said we had a glass Socialist Jesus in our church window, but Jerry was a real one. Jerry was a real Socialist."

"I wanted to believe in *something*." Steve snapped this as if I had been arguing with him.

The need to believe in something.

Mrs. Farmer believed in Knowing the Truth.

Josie Dowell, Hope Dowell, Willard Dowell, and Edward Dowell, the four original Placer County Family Members, had believed in the Brotherhood of Man. But they had needed to come to Northern California to practice it.

"Talk and blather," Steve said.

To our right, train thunder began to gather.

"I hate his goddamn pious talk."

After a minute Steve went on. "French Ford is an enclosed community. Do you know what that means?"

"Of course."

"We've had special rules. The Dowells have had special rules."

I nodded. A magic mountain; we lived on a magic mountain. In the rest of the world, you could not get away with stealing groceries, screwing beside your grandparents' grave, practicing Socialism.

"Talk." Steve began to rise to his feet on the pile of lumber. "Sure and forever," his voice rose, took on an affected Irish accent, "sure and forever, that bastard charms the darlin' birds out of the darlin' trees . . ." Up the canyon the train shrieked; its noise gathered around us, bouncing from rock to rock.

Steve waved his arms. "I hate his goddamn Irish blather." Instead of deepening his voice to compete with the train, he made it higher, into a falsetto shout. "My brothers an' people, my frens an' voters, all of yez that can drag yer ass to th' polls on that great come an' get it day," he waved his arms. "I'm here to tell ya, the American people . . . will stand firm . . ." He shifted balance, grabbed at the sky. "THE WORKING MAN WILL *NEVER* . . . GIVE IN TO THE STRESSES . . . Americans will never, never . . ." he was singing now, "NEVER WILL BE SLAVES."

The train appeared around the bend blinking its light. The engineer leaned out of the cab and waved at us.

7

Sybil was better. Her trip into the mine had accomplished what experiences like that are supposed to. Evva's nursing book had a chapter about mock suicide, about how the person expends the suicide energy and never needs to do that again.

"Just the same," my father said, "you promised her a party."

I didn't want to have a party for Sybil. I was cross at her. "Don't you think it's odd that David McCracken rescued us?"

"Not particularly. He used to be a levelheaded child."

Daddy was being difficult. He knew that what interested me was the drama of the two colliding legends: *Lost in the Mine* and *The Runaway Boy*.

"We'll have a formal party," Daddy said. "You'll wear your purple dress. I'll wear my tux. Mrs. Farmer will make mock turtle soup."

I said, "Oh God," and went upstairs to write to Steve, who was back in San Francisco.

Dear Steve:
You would hate the party with all the dotty neediest
Dowells . . .

I stared at this for a while and ripped it in half. It invoked the worst of Steve and the worst of me.

I got out the box in which I kept Steve's letters and reread them.

Daddy was nicer than I was. Evva was nicer than I was. Indiana used to be nicer.

I decided to write to Indiana.

Dear Indiana:
Some Russian writer wrote a book called Notes from Underground. *I have been thinking about you a lot lately, and so I decided to write you a letter to* Underground. *Forgive the macabre touch, Indy, but to a certain extent you asked for it.*

I sat on the window seat with the window open to admit the herbal smells and mockingbird chant, and wrote this letter to Indiana on a ruled yellow pad that I held on my knee.

Indy, we miss you.
We think about you a lot.

I had partly expected to be crying while I wrote this, and I wasn't. One up for me.

I think about you in snatches, when I am not expecting to.

I turned my pencil around and read the green writing on it. I wasn't a pencil-chewer. Too bad. Pencil-chewing would have given me something to do in the interstices of this letter.

These snatches of memory are side-views of you, as if I

*were seeing you out of the corner of my eye. Do you
remember that picture they took of you for the high school
magazine? You were twirling so your skirts stood out?
That year you certainly had good legs.*

(Don't imply that she used to get fat.)

*And the way you would laugh, and then ask a question,
and then laugh again, as if there were something wrong
with the question, and of course no one was going to
answer it, anyway. Or the way you wrote notes to absolutely everybody, in colored ink on posied paper: "Dear
Auntie Sybil: This is just to wish you the happiest Mother's
Day ever."* (And Sybil wasn't your, nor anybody's,
mother.) *Or to my father, a card, hand-made and with a
cut-out of a Campbell Soup Kid on the corner: "Thank
you, thank you; my nose doesn't run any more."* (Daddy
had removed your adenoids.) *You even sent notes to me,
Indy, and I was five years younger; I was young enough
that you might perfectly well not have noticed me: "Dear
Grace: We're all so proud of you. Delivering the Memorial
Day adress!"*

(There are two *d*'s in address, Indy.)

(And there was that quality of need both in the notes
and in the voice, a pleading rise in inflection, with a question at the end. "How *are* you today?" Translation: Don't
jump me for asking. My intentions are good. I'm not trying to pry. What did Steve think of that, I wonder, what
did he make of that need? Attractive at first, and then too
much, I would guess.)

*Indy, since I am not going to mail this letter ever, not
even at the interstellar, intergalactic universal post office, I
can remember that sometimes you used to be beautiful and*

sometimes you used not to be. You had that non-Dowell tendency to put on weight; for goodness sake, how ever did you manage that? So that sometimes those narrow Dowell face-bones were swathed in chins and the rayed green eyes mounded by pink flesh. Though God knows you were skinny enough just before you did all your wrist-slitting and stuff.

(My literary style is disintegrating.)

You must have sent notes to Steve. Steve must have a good collection of notes. Even if he never saw your diary.

Maybe Steve wouldn't save the notes.

I have reached the end of this legal-sized page.

Turn the page and write on the back? Use next page? Stop? I inspected the pencil label again. What was Ticonderoga and why did they put it on pencils?

Indy had had a tendency, too, to lose buttons and the stitching out of hems, to wear a skirt that was so tight it didn't zip or one that was so loose it sat over one hipbone. And alternately, the next day, to get all dressed up and twirl her skirts and have her picture taken. And be surprised when you said, "Indy, you certainly are looking good."

She collected facts: Indy's little-known facts: "If you do *it,* you know, *sex,* standing on your head, it will be a boy. If you want to disappear ever, run away, from the police or your parents, just kind of fade out and not be noticed, go to Reno. In Reno, nobody ever really looks at you."

That one had seemed to me to have genuine practical application; I had thought about it since.

I stared some more at my page, wrote *Goodbye Indiana and good luck* across the quarter inch remaining at the bottom, and ripped the page off and twisted it into a long spill.

Ultimately, it seemed to be the fat Indiana whom I was remembering. And that wasn't the way I wanted it to be.

"Listen," Daddy said, "Listen; it's going to be great; we'll put the big Italian pure-wax candles in the chandelier . . ."

"It sounds silly, Daddy; it sounds like a joke."

I really did suspect my father of a kind of joke in planning Sybil's party, of secretly playing the part of The Arranger in a French classical play. Then I looked at him and thought about it, and decided *no*. Daddy had his kind and helpful side. It wasn't his fault that his enjoyment seemed self-conscious and forced. In many ways he really was nicer than I was.

I asked that Evva be included in the guest list; she could wear her senior prom dress, which she had worn only once. Lloyd McCracken wasn't going to take her anyplace suitable for the blue silk faille with puffed sleeves and peplum.

And Sybil was ready for another foraging excursion into Mother's closet. I visualized the scene in the cedar-lined room, hot, smelling enclosed and yet crisp, Sybil and I walking along the lines of dresses, with me saying, "This one, Sybil," or "How about this here; it's hardly been worn." I began to get interested in this party.

Except for Steve's mother, now. I wasn't looking forward to a whole evening with Steve's mother, Myrtle, whose conversation was a series of gentle protests, as if she were telling you something very interesting: Steve's dog had knocked over the garbage can . . . "And I am a widow; things are harder when you are a widow; people take advantage of you . . ."

Myrtle's brown eyes were surrounded by yellowed whites and she had wobbly jowls, like the cheek pockets of a hamster.

I probably wasn't going to have mother-in-law trouble, not the kind where the mother is a rival to the wife. "My father died to get away from her," Steve said. "*I* had to wait to go to college."

"Didn't there used to a time when you liked her?"

He had looked at me with his blank stare, the one that implied you had said something childish. "She must have been nice before your dad died." How would my own mother have turned out?

Steve's face closed up. "I can't remember."

During Sybil's dinner I stared at my relatives and tried to decide how peculiar they actually were. Daddy was outlining his plans for my wedding: the wedding party would march through town; this was a charming rural custom; they did it in Europe. "In some parts," Sybil agreed, squinting at the Italian wax candles. Her sleeveless black dress showed a lot of aged pale Sybil. "Good grief," Evva objected, curving athletically inside her blue faille. Indiana's husband Phil simply smiled; he looked freckled and normal, not as if he had just buried his suicidal wife.

Sybil had gotten us to invite Lenny Barr Dowell, a Dowell cousin who lived down Deep Creek Road with seventeen cats. Lenny worked in the French Ford General Store. He was creased and brown, and wore a gray silk shirt, probably borrowed from Daddy.

Sybil said, "I keep thinking Indy is here." She aimed her hawk gaze at the tureen that Indiana had liked, the one with the porcelain cow on its cover. Daddy was ladling from it now, leaning forward, king of his family, dishing up Mrs. Farmer's beef in red wine. "Mock turtle soup," Daddy had worried, "beef in red wine; I'm not sure they'll *accord?*" Daddy was an artist. A doctor, sometimes, is a kind of artist.

I've lived with these people all my life, and I don't understand them. "Indy was creative; people didn't know that," I said to Sybil. "Did you admire her?"

"*Admire* her?" Sybil hunched shoulder bones against black chiffon. "How can you ask such questions? What is the matter with you?"

"Your Auntie Syb *loved* Indiana," Lenny Barr translated. "You know, with that pure kind of love. Like the Bible calls for."

Mrs. Farmer, sitting with us now that the beef had been served, touched her garnet beads. "You should love your neighbor as yourself. With the same kind of love."

"Indy wrote things," I said. "Some people didn't know that."

Sybil was still angry. "I knew that she did. I knew that she would write. When I saw that baby toddling unscathed out of the flames I knew she was *destined*."

Sybil was talking about The Fire. The Fire had happened three weeks after Mother died. I was fifteen months old for The Fire; I didn't remember it. It is hard to keep in the forefront of your mind a fire that occurred when you were a baby.

I closed my eyes and tried to imagine the wall of flames six hundred feet high, so hot it had blistered the paint off the sign on the General Store, that red electric curtain, a red barrier across the road out of French Ford. History in French Ford; history for Steve and for Steve's mother. Sybil once told me that The Fire ate Steve's father "like a leaf in a bonfire."

I looked at Myrtle, who didn't mind talking about all this. "I bet he walked into it on purpose." Steve had told me this about his father. He usually avoided the subject.

All of us settled into our boeuf bourguignon. "It is delicious," Sybil pronounced. Daddy asked, "The carrots not too done?" and Sybil said, "They are perfect."

"You were there?" I asked Lenny Barr.

Lenny turned his friendly, seamed face. Like most Dowell relatives, he had blue eyes; his were less green than mine. "The Fire? *Uh*-huh. You betcha."

"Tell us."

"Yeah?" Lenny appeared to think. "That was some hell of a fire."

"So tell us."

"It was real, real . . ." He searched for a word.

I was surprised when Phil intervened. "Indiana talked about it."

A moment's silence. "Indy was only a baby," I objected.

"She was five. She remembered it. She saw a tree explode. She saw Marcus go."

I stared at Phil. Marcus was Steve's father.

"She saw him standing on the rim. The fire made a finger, a pouch, and reached out and pulled him in." Phil ran a hand over his neat brown hair. He had never before this talked to me of anything more dangerous than insurance, or recipes for direct-mail success, or, once in the

56

General Store, of the best kind of paint for a plywood gazebo.

He didn't seem to feel us watching and went on talking, "Like a wave engulfing a swimmer."

"Except," Sybil amended critically, "the angle would be different."

Myrtle sighed, and Mrs. Farmer told her, "I'm sorry, Myrtle darling."

"In a way you don't ever get used to it," Myrtle said. "People keep telling me to accept it. How can you accept it?"

Myrtle had tipped her head back; her posture didn't look self-pitying: she looked like the drawing of Joan of Arc in my storybook; I was pretty sure Myrtle hadn't ever seen that drawing. She turned yellowed eyes at me. "Steve accuses me. Maybe you don't know *that* side of Steve."

Myrtle, I know that side all right.

"Indy remembered the trees, too," Phil said. "She used to talk about a tree going up, like a giant rocket."

We were silent, scraping beef bourguignon. "You know what she said?" Phil asked. "She told me she ran down the road crying, and she met Steve and he said, 'Hey, Indy, were you scared? I was scared, too.' He said, 'Hey, Indy, maybe it'll all be all right in a while, do you think it will?' And know what she said? She said she thinks his father had just been killed, just then. That just before he said this to her he'd seen his own father killed.

"Indy thinks of Steve in a special way," Phil added speculatively.

Myrtle sighed again and I stared at Evva, who returned my gaze. She had noticed it, too; *Phil speaks of Indiana in the present tense.* Evva reached out and patted Myrtle's hand.

"The point is," Sybil said, "when we have these conversations I keep remembering Indiana. She really loved to speculate about things."

A long time after I saw Steve and Indiana together in the middle of Indiana's kitchen floor I thought of asking him, "Why did you kiss Indiana?" and also, "Did you love Indiana?" But I never asked either of these questions; I knew there wasn't any answer to the first, and I was pretty sure the second answer would be no.

There are people who stave off the darkness inside them with excitement. If they stop gesturing and singing and shooting off rockets for a moment that central pit at their core, like a trap dug by an ant lion, will start to revolve and pull them under. I understood this because I had a few of these feelings myself. But nothing like what Steve must have had. Maybe the difference between us was as simple as the difference between seeing your father burned up before your eyes and having your mother die of pneumonia; maybe it was that the non-Dowell halves of us were different and my non-Dowell genes were stronger than his non-Dowell ones.

"Does Steve love me?" I asked Evva, who said, "Steve doesn't love anybody." Then she looked sorry. "He loves you as much as he can."

My father said the same thing, only differently. I caught him in one of his literary moments. "Listen, Chiclet, do you know the poem . . . ?"

"No poems." But he went right on and quoted: "Ah,

58

love, let us be true/ to one another! for the world, which seems/ To lie before us like a land of dreams/ Hath really neither love nor joy nor light . . ."

I said, "Oh, swell," and he said, "Well, that's what it's like," and started to add something about, "for Steve, especially." But I didn't stop to listen; I was already on my way upstairs.

8

The craziest Dowell was Sybil, the most appealing Dowell Indiana, the most phlegmatic one Lenny Barr . . . and the most versatile was my father.

"Almost a genius," Sybil had said during one of her periods of admiring Daddy. "Well, close to a genius. Do you know that he once got a taxidermist's license?"

"And then never taxidermed."

"Also archeology."

I said that you didn't get a license to be an archeologist.

"A true Renaissance Man." Sybil sighed.

I went to the encyclopedia and looked up *Renaissance Man*. After I had read the article I agreed with Sybil that Daddy was one, but I pretended not to agree. "The Renaissance Man was a man of letters."

Maybe it was the fact that Daddy addressed me as Babe that made me feel he wasn't a man of letters.

Daddy had brought my dark, elegant mother to French Ford from San Francisco. She was rumored to have been rebellious.

"The heart of the heartland," Daddy said. "The true West, the true America." He meant French Ford, which he admired. "Don't knock it," he would say, "think about it. The true America, the genuine American rural proletariat, is right here in French Ford." Daddy had written four pamphlets about the American Rural Proletariat; he tried hard to keep up the Dowell Socialist tradition.

My father called the French Ford old ladies Babe, just the way he called me Babe. They loved it. That darling Doctor Dowell.

"Hey, Babe, hi Babe; how's Babe?" Lloyd McCracken circled me on his motorcycle. "Does Daddy whack it into Babe like he does to all the other chicks in town?"

Lloyd said this while he was mad at Evva; afterwards he apologized.

I wanted to ask Lloyd what he had meant, but I didn't. I thought, the hell with it. I went and looked at the picture of my mother, dark and small and not resembling a Dowell at all.

Maybe he started calling people Babe after she died.

"You don't have to worry; you've got your family," Evva said. "But I don't have anybody. I've got to live in now. So I *took* some money out of my Nursing Fund. I've got to live Now."

Even saying "sure you do" seemed patronizing, so I kept quiet. I felt guilty about the fact that Evva wanted to be a nurse and couldn't do it; she had been admitted to the program at Sacramento General a year ago, but her family wouldn't give her the money for books and uniforms. She was saving her telephone company salary for that.

"Dad thinks I should get married to somebody, anybody. Just so he has a job and only one head . . . Do you like the player? It's like yours; it does six records."

She and I were in her room, with the ice and the vodka. She was alternately sewing on her bridesmaid's dress, a blue chiffon with blue lace trim, and staring moodily at her drink.

I took a sip of mine; it tasted harsh and, for some reason, real. "All the rest of my life, whenever I have vodka, I'll think of you, Evva."

"Thanks, *loads*. Where are you going to be, that you'll be thinking of me?"

"In San Francisco. Married to Steve."

"That's not exactly going to remove you out of my sphere of influence, is it?" She turned the record player down.

There was a pause while she sewed, tugging and pulling to keep something even. "I guess I should tell you. I'm going out with Lloyd again."

When I didn't comment she said, "If you can *marry* Stone-face, I can *go out* with Lloyd."

Evva knew what I thought of Lloyd McCracken. "Sometimes you get along with Steve fine."

"And sometimes I don't. Well, I'll shut up; I see why you like him; all those brains and no potatoes; just watch out it doesn't get to be too much."

"What do you mean, no potatoes?" I asked suspiciously.

"It's just a song . . . Christ." Evva had snagged her thread, which was unusual for her; she was very neat in her performance of mechanical tasks. "Lloyd is taking me to Auburn to see *Lost Horizon*."

Lloyd must really have liked Evva. *Lost Horizon* wasn't his kind of entertainment.

"And it's okay that Duke rescued you from the mine. But you sure do get all the action." She sewed and sighed some more. "I hope I can stay out of the back seat of Lloyd's car."

"How can you?"

"What do you mean, how *can* I?"

"Well, if you did it before, you have to do it again."

She didn't contradict me. I thought, Maybe better the back seat of Lloyd's Ford than nothing, than negative nothing, than that thumping exotic Steve engine that can't, that won't, that doesn't explain.

Evva started talking about nursing school. If she saved another two hundred dollars she could start classes in January. She could move into the nurses' residence; they were saving a room for her. You were supposed to bring your own bedspread; she had chosen a pink and white seersucker one out of the Sears catalogue. "And my daddy can have the epileptic fit to end all fits, and I hope it kills him . . . Oh hell, I've stuck myself." She threw the bridesmaid's dress on the floor and put her finger in her mouth. "Dad put a hex on me."

"You should drip blood on the snow and wish for a daughter with red, red lips . . ."

"Wouldn't that be nifty." She held the finger under the reading lamp. "Hey, listen, Grace, speaking of hexes . . ."

"Hexes?"

"You remember what Sybil said about Felicia the Futurist?"

Felicia the Futurist lived in a log house outside Amos,

the next town up the road from French Ford. She made her living by "consultations," which she advertised in the *Auburn Herald-Tribune* along with her title, *Felicia the Futurist*. Her name was universally mispronounced in Placer County: Fleesha.

"What did Sybil say about Fleesha?"

"About you should have a consultation." Evva picked the dress off the floor and began searching for the place where she had stopped sewing. "She goes on and on about it."

Sybil had raised this idea with me only once; after that she had evidently shifted her campaign to Evva. I had gotten cross with her because she had coupled the fortune-telling suggestion with reminders that Indiana's death was an ill omen for my wedding.

"I must say"—Evva bent over her work—"I'd like to. It would be nifty. I've wanted to for a long while now."

"She's just an ordinary old woman."

"She doesn't see everybody. She has to *want* to see you. If you told her you were getting married she would. Want to see you." She snicked the end of her thread with her teeth.

"You look like somebody's mother. Sure. Let's see if Fleesha will talk to us. But don't tell Sybil."

I didn't want Sybil crowing over me. Sybil loved to feel that she had gotten the better of you.

Evva and I rode to Fleesha's cabin on horse-back.

Both of us could drive, but someone who sees you driving a car thinks you're going in a specific direction. If you're on a horse perhaps you're just ambling. We didn't want to advertise that we were seeing Fleesha.

"Now, dear, you'll not ride her too fast?" Mrs. Farmer had asked, smoothing Hattie's gray, drooping muzzle.

Hattie had splayed feet and an indented, knobbed back. She traveled in first gear only; I leaned forward on her neck, kicked my foot back and forth, and read the signs Fleesha had put up along the fence. They were all the same kind of sign: POSTED, PRIVATE PROPERTY, KEEP OUT. "Where does she get them from?" I asked Evva. EXTREME FIRE DANGER. LIVE WIRES.

"Colfax Hardware." We passed SWIMMING PRO-HIBITED; was that supposed to be funny? It contained the same negative message as the other signs.

Evva was scared about this visit, I could tell. She was hardly talking at all. I wasn't scared; at least, I didn't think I was. Was I supposed to ask Fleesha a question? I thought of a possible question and rejected it. Could I just say, "Fleesha, will I find happiness?"

That was the sort of inquiry that got you into trouble. You were asked to define happiness, and when you did so it was all wrong.

Daddy had been to see Fleesha and wouldn't really tell me what she had said; he hedged with, well I'll be meeting new people. I'll have interesting new ideas. Big deal, I had told him, oh, big deal. He said he had visited her because she was a Placer County Custom, and he was interested in Placer County Customs.

Fleesha's log house was on stilts and had a steeply pitched roof with a scalloped cornice around it. That part of the ambience was fine; it had the eccentricity I had been hoping for. But Fleesha herself looked just the way she should not have. She was fat and round; she had a pink print dress and white hair and wire-rimmed glasses. The only unusual thing about her was an enormous topaz ring on her right index finger; she flashed this when she gestured.

Evva and I sat in her living room, Evva on a green-checked couch, I on a chair. I stared at a painting of a shingled house by a winding river; it had a label: "Under the Spreading Chestnut Tree."

"Who goes first?" I asked Evva.

I hadn't spoken loudly, but Fleesha heard us in the kitchen. "Oh, no, dear," she called, clinking something against something (she was making tea), "*I* decide that." Her high Placer County voice got authoritative.

I liked that better and sat back to admire the second picture, also better. It showed the sinking of the *Titanic*. The iceberg loomed across three-quarters of the picture; the ship was small and sharply canted, its nose pointing skyward. The artist had decorated the black night with a shooting star.

Fleesha stood over us, massaging her hands, while we drank tea. Then she aimed the topaz at Evva. "I'll see you first, dear." The ring pointed at me. "Then you."

I settled into a maple chair. Evva followed Fleesha through a door, which shut authoritatively; it was being locked. I slid onto the middle of my spine and looked around at the pine-panelled walls and high-pitched ceiling. On the coffee table was a display of magazines the size and shape of *The Reader's Digest*. One of these was called *Your Health*. One was called *Today's Gardens*. Oh, well. I got up and rummaged through the maple bookcase. *Ra-*

mona. Joyce Kilmer's poems. Finally, between *Lad, A Dog* and *Girl of the Limberlost* I found what I was looking for: *Crossing the Mind-Matter Boundary, The Seventh Inner World, The Future, An Open Book.* I took *The Future* back to my chair. It was written in an exhortatory style that I associated with ads at the back of the Sunday comics: "Anyone, by the right feeling combination of Loving Touch and Total Integral Empathy can enter the subject's force field and intuit the valleys and peaks of the soul's prospective country." Inscribed in the margin beside this in a round, school-teacherly hand was "Interesting, but primitive."

I was admiring this appraisal when the door made its unlocking noise and Evva walked in.

"Well?" I asked.

"See for yourself." She slumped on the couch and grabbed *Your Health.*

"You didn't like it."

"I didn't say that." She buried her head in the magazine. I returned to *The Future.* "You can do it if you will set your Energy/Will firmly on the plane of Total Acceptance . . ." The door opened again. Fleesha appeared, plump arms folded, looking as if she had just baked a nice pie.

"Come in, Grace dear . . . Leave your wristwatch on the coffee table."

"My watch?"

"It's the wrong kind of metal."

The watch was a birthday Bulova, a gift from my father; it said "Gold Plated Base Metal" across the back. Maybe it was the phrase "base metal" that Fleesha hadn't liked. Maybe she had read right through the watch face and found that word *base* and hated it. I unhooked the watch

67

and laid it on the table, and followed her through a door, which she locked.

We went down a hallway into an apparently windowless room. There was a table and two straight chairs. A kerosene lamp sat on the table; the air was heavy with oily fumes.

"You're not menstruating, dear?"

"No."

The topaz gestured at a chair. I sat down.

Silence while Fleesha brushed off the table. It looked clean, but she made sweeping motions with her fat hands, flexed her fingers as if she were about to play the piano. "Do you know how this works?"

"No." I toyed with the word *mumbo-jumbo*.

"All right, now." She turned up the kerosene lamp. "Just fix your eyes on the flame. Reach out and take my hands. No, no. RELAX and take my hands. Let your mind go. Watch the light."

I decided, all right, I'll go along, what else am I here for? Mumbo-jumbo, hocus-pocus. Stuff. Nonsense.

"STOP thinking." The command had real head-nurse force. "Make your mind blank. Think of an open space . . . You are in a wide space . . . you are falling . . . All around you is space. Your arms are stretched out. You are turning in a circle. Your legs are spread; your arms are spread. You have no power over your arms and legs. You weigh nothing. You're falling, you're falling faster . . ."

Dreams and visions are hard to describe. The pit that I went into was at first bright and then dark, a machine pulled me down. It swallowed me. One minute I resisted and heard Fleesha's voice; the next minute I was inside the noise: a fan, a refrigerator motor, a locomotive, someone's voice, a heartbeat . . .

When I came to I was lying on the floor. Fleesha squatted beside me, pulling at my belt. "Hold still. You've wet your pants."

I turned my face away from her. Tears seeped out on either side of my face and trickled toward my hair.

"That happens often, dear. It's perfectly normal. We'll have you out of these jeans in a jiffy."

She tugged my jeans and underpants off and went away with them; I heard a washing-machine start somewhere. When she returned she had a blanket, which she tucked around me, and a wedge-shaped pillow, which she put under my head. She sat down on the floor and lit a cigarette. "Now, let's talk."

"What in hell did you do?"

"I hypnotized you."

"You were supposed to predict my future."

"I know." She expelled smoke. "You are more sensitive than you let yourself think."

"Oh, cut it out."

"Your father is a better friend than you let him be."

"Bull. Shit."

"Don't use that language, please. You are forgetting things that will help you if you can remember them."

I didn't answer this one.

"There are rocks ahead. Sharp currents."

"What in hell does that mean?"

"It means danger. Danger, dear. Real, serious danger."

"Double, double, toil and trouble . . ."

"Mock all you like; you'll find out. Marriage equals

danger. Not marrying equals danger. Decision equals danger."

"So does living. When will my pants be done?"

Fleesha went out of the room and I sat up and blew my nose. "Can I have a cigarette?" I asked when she came back.

"I see someone who can't breathe," she said, handing me her pack of Lucky Strikes.

"That's my mother. She died of pneumonia. Anybody in French Ford could have told you that."

"There is someone else. I see someone who can't move."

"That's my mother, still. Jesus."

"Someone different, dear." Fleesha seemed unperturbed.

"How long for my pants?"

"Five more minutes."

I had trouble getting the cigarette lighted. Fleesha held a match for me. She sat cross-legged on the floor, hunched comfortably forward. Well, I thought, no other old lady in Placer County could do that.

"I know what you think of me," she said.

"No, you don't."

"You think I'm an ordinary old woman who has read a book on hypnotism. And I know what you wanted me to do for you."

"What?"

"You wanted me to tell you what was going to happen, year by year, for the next ten years."

"I'm not that childish."

"You wanted me to tell you specific things. I don't do that. The results are terrible. I'll get your clothes." She rose, using both hands to push herself up, like any other Placer County old lady.

She came back with my blue jeans and underpants and leaned against the wall, puffing at her cigarette, to watch me while I struggled into them. "That kerosene is giving me a headache," I said.

"Listen, dear, I'll say three things. The first is that your life's pattern is getting and losing. That's your life's design. Getting. Losing." She blew smoke at me in a straight jet.

"That's everybody's life's pattern, for creep's sake."

"Second: the man you plan to marry will do you harm." I didn't answer this. I was fastening my belt.

"And a final thing, dear. Read the papers."

"The *news*papers? What in hell for?"

"For practice." She eyed the blue jeans. "Those cuffs are still damp."

"The hell with it." I was still thinking about that last one.

"Well, how was it?" Evva asked on the way back.

"Oh, pretty much *nada y pues nada*."

"What does that mean?"

"Nothing. I forgot you don't like Hemingway. It means 'nothing.' What about you?"

"The usual. A dark man. And money. A trip over water."

"I guess maybe I did better than you did."

9

Evva told me that I was spoiled, and I agreed; she said, all you Dowells think you're the Kings and Queens of Placer County, and I agreed, that's right, we are; then Evva, losing speed, said that God had been unfair in handing us so large a share of the looks (and brains, too, I guess, she went on, though as far as wits go, none of you has enough to come home from the store); *but,* Evva told me, relenting, *you've* had your share of bad luck; all of you, I mean; but *you,* especially.

"All Dowells have bad luck," I told her. "They do it to themselves."

"*You* didn't do anything," said Evva, completely partisan by now. "*You* were just a baby."

I was fourteen months old when my mother died. According to local legend it was the quickest case of pneumonia my father had ever seen. "He was quite distracted," Sybil said. "Quite rigidly distracted."

I was never sure where Sybil got her vocabulary from.

"What was I like?"

"You were a baby." Sybil paused and seemed to realize this didn't cover all possibilities. "You were supposed to have been very bright."

Sybil had never had any children; this was probably a good thing. This particular conversation took place in the diggings; Sybil and I were sitting on the two lawn chairs she kept near her Buick, for receiving guests in, for relaxing in. "I believe you were able to do something quite unusual for your age." She squinted toward the white gravel horizon. "Perhaps you could read."

"Not at fourteen months, Aunt Sybil."

"Then maybe you could talk."

Mrs. Farmer was more specific and said that I had had a vocabulary of one hundred and forty-two words. "She counted them, the cute thing," Mrs. Farmer said, meaning my mother. "That's how I remember. You called yourself Gace."

I had tried to imagine it, Gace in her room, the same one I had now, with the blue roses and the window seat, practicing her vocabulary, her mother in the next room, dying faster than any pneumonia patient Daddy had ever had.

Dowells, even Dowells by marriage, don't do things halfway.

Now, at nineteen, I had no memory of my mother, but I did have numerous evidences of her: her clothes, her cedar closet, an envelope of pictures speckled gray to mauve, curling at the corners, featuring a dark, fine-boned woman bent over a frilled blob of baby, thin white-boned hand clutching Baby's middle. My pictured mother inclined over me so protectively and with such maternal grace that the two of us could have been posed for a nativity group.

I had looked at these pictures often while I sat on the

window seat. I remember sitting that way one fall day when I was about eleven; I held the pictures up to the light, evaluated them, set them aside in a stack next to me. An autumn storm slammed against the window as if an enormous wet sheet were being slapped against the glass. Steve came in and sat beside me. He picked up a picture and said, "She was beautiful." That was the day I decided that my mother had not wanted to die, that she had been sorry to leave me; I could even fantasize her looking down on me from some indistinct blue place above the cloud cover that was pelting French Ford. She felt sorry for me, she loved me; she would help me if she could. She was not, as I had dreamed one night, happily established in a house behind the Post Office, raising another family, none of whom looked like me.

"I couldn't make him get off the bed." Sybil was describing the day Mother had died. "Your father lay on top of the covers, half turned toward her, holding her hand. 'I'll be up in a minute, Syb,' he said. That was the first time. But a half hour later he wouldn't answer me. He made a noise . . ." I could see Sybil's speculative side taking over; she touched her throat. "Somewhere low in here, I think, an animal noise . . ." She patted my arm. "Don't worry, my dear, your father has recovered. As much as anyone does."

I nodded. Daddy had other problems now, not those ones. "Tell about *me*."

"You were in the next room." I, too, had been in bed; I had sat in my crib turning the pages of a linen book. As Sybil entered I aimed a finger at a picture; then I held out my arms to be picked up. "You smelled a little," she told me, consideringly. "You were only a baby."

* * *

Daddy had had his first heart attack right after Mother died, Sybil said, and then another one, and there had also been a recent something . . .

"Why doesn't he tell me?"

"Perhaps he thinks you shouldn't be worried."

After a while she added, "I think he's ashamed."

I went to my eighth-grade teacher who asked, "Why do you ask, Grace?"

"I'm writing a story."

"Well, sometimes it's serious and sometimes it's not. Who in the story has the heart attack?"

A middle-aged woman, I said, and Mrs. Fitch told me heart attacks were worse for women than for men. She suggested I make it something milder, like ulcers.

She didn't give me the usual adult speech about not dwelling on sad things. She was a young, energetic teacher and was interested in sad things, too.

Sybil described the first heart attack. Daddy had clutched his arm. His face turned gray.

"Gray?"

"Yes. Well, almost. Pale purple, actually."

Pale purple was worse.

"He grabbed the back of a chair. Leaned against it. He said, 'I am having a heart attack.' "

"He would know if he was. He's a doctor."

"My third husband had five."

That was no help. Sybil's third husband was the one who finally died.

I didn't say, Sybil, will he have another one? I thought of going to Daddy and asking about this. There were two ways he might respond. Maybe he would aim his slightly

75

popped eyes at me and say, Why, honey-babe, that's some question; what brings on that question, anyway? But not to dwell on it, huh? Or there might, if I caught him at the wrong moment, be a spasm near the eyes, and he might admit everything: Yes, I had an attack, Babe; yes, didn't want to scare you . . . and then he might give me a medical synopsis: this could happen; that could happen. But the medical synopsis would be an edited one.

I asked Steve what I should do. Steve and Daddy were close; they were the town intellectuals, the town radical thinkers. They got together and argued over the books Steve brought from the San Francisco Soviet Bookstore. When I asked him my question Steve smiled his Steve smile and repeated that I spent my life with people older than I.

"Yes, but what do I *do?*"

"Marry me."

I had taken biology in school just to learn about hearts, but learning about them didn't help: "the strongest muscle in the body"—until something goes wrong—then, "delicate, fine . . . minor changes can upset."

Steve wouldn't talk to me about it. "Marry me."

I told him I never knew when he was serious, and he didn't answer me.

Further letters from Steve:

Dearest Grace:
There was a long article in the paper today about why people jump off the Golden Gate Bridge.
I would have thought they did this because the bridge is artistically and technically perfect, and there is a human-

simian instinct to sully what is perfect. But, no; it seems it
has to do with the concept of "West."

People move West looking for something better, and
each step of the way it is the same; the place is different but
the same problems are waiting, and finally the people
reach San Francisco, all white and blue and as Western as
anything can be, but with the same problems, exactly the
same ones. And there is that bridge, with its Pacific Ocean
and its sunset.

So what does this do for those of us who were raised in
the West; for whom West is Here, not There?

Write to me; I miss you.

(A postcard)

Grace dear, I have been having really weird dreams;
they are not only in color but in sensation, specific feelings
like the chill of an ice cube, pin-pricks from dream pins;
last night it was fire; I had put my hand in the fire and
watched while the palm shriveled and crisped; you had
asked me to do that, but you wouldn't really ask for such a
thing, would you, Grace?

s/ Burned Child

Grazia:

How can you be a Dowell and be so free of despair? It is
not natural. Un-nachral. Crime against nature. Contra na-
tura. An optimistic Dowell.

Grace, in a fit of self-perception it dawns on me that it is
selfish to burden you with these scab-pickings.

Jerry Shaughnessey would not like me this way at all.

S.

(A political leaflet with handwritten notes at top and bottom)

(Note at top):
Messiah returned as middle-aged beer-drinking Irishman

(Text of leaflet, a montage of newspaper headlines):
JERRY SHAUGHNESSEY
CATHOLIC, WORKING CLASS, LIBERAL
JERRY CARES

J FOR $\begin{cases} \text{JERRY} \\ \text{JOBS} \end{cases}$

(Note at bottom):
Darling Grace:
Please do not forget that you are going to marry me.
                              Love, always love.

10

It was the week after our visit to Fleesha. Evva was at her telephone station, flipping switches and talking into a round receptor balanced in front of her chin. I sat on the floor with my back to the wall. I was smoking again, using a coffee-can lid as an ashtray.

I said, "Evva?"

Evva said, "Huh?"

"Steve has done something."

Evva clicked and snapped for a while and then ducked her head to show she was ready to deal with me. "What now?"

"These cigarettes taste awful."

"So don't smoke."

"Quit being logical."

She returned to her switchboard. After a while she swept her hand down it with a conclusive gesture. "Okay. What?"

"Steve sent David McCracken up here."

"David? You mean Duke? Whatever for?"

It was going to be difficult to explain this to Evva; I hadn't been able to explain it to myself. At one o'clock yesterday there had been a rattle at the front screen door. I had seen, outlined by the bright noonday haze, a vaguely familiar figure; I opened the door, squinted, blinked. The person said, "It's me. David McCracken."

Duke McCracken, the runaway boy of Placer County. Didn't they teach you in college to say, "It is I"? No, they didn't. "Come in."

David followed me into the living room and sat on the edge of a green chair. "I'm here on a funny errand."

"Uh?"

"Steve, I guess he couldn't get away . . . Maybe he wanted it to be a special surprise." David was having trouble with this formulation. He stared at his knobbed hands, which held a box of some light-absorbing material, perhaps velvet.

"I'm supposed to give you this. It's . . . your engagement ring."

And he handed over the box, which was indeed of velvet, with a snap lid. I opened it, there was a ring shaped like a flower: a spray, one large diamond and six small ones. The design was old-fashioned and strange; I liked it a lot.

I started to say thank you to David McCracken, but that seemed like the wrong response; after all, he hadn't chosen the ring. At least, I didn't think he had.

He leaned forward to look. After a while he asked, "Are you going to put it on?"

I did that, third finger, left hand, and laid the box on the table. The spray of stones gathered light. There was another minute of silence. It was uncomfortable, but not terribly so; David managed silence well; his posture and

the inclination of his head showed interest. A proxy engagement. There had been a picture in *The Sacramento Bee*
of a soldier marrying his Japanese girl friend in a proxy
wedding. The proxy bride hadn't been Japanese; she had
been blonde, with light eyes. Probably she was the girl next
door.

I felt newly aware of this room I was so used to: green
walls with undersea glow, shelves of books, also glowing
green.

Evva did something to her switchboard so it stopped
making noises, although it still lit up. "Don't ask *me* what
Steve was up to," she said. "Steve and I are as different as
night and day. We're at the far ends of the spectrum. We're
opposites."

Several red lights starred the switchboard. Evva surveyed them moodily. "Were you embarrassed?"

"Not really."

"You know in stories . . ."

"Yes?"

"They slip the wrong person into the marriage bed and
the other one never notices."

Maybe I should have been insulted by this flight of fantasy; instead it struck me as funny. I began to laugh, and so
did Evva. Before we were finished laughing her board had
made a red and green pattern that looked like the highway
on Saturday night.

Finally I had said to David, "It's funny having you here
. . ."

In response to some movement by him I said, "It's okay,
though; I like it," and turned my hand so the ring flashed.

He said, "Well, I guess I better be going." But I sug-

gested iced tea, and after that I suggested a walk. The walk
started out simply as an amble up Main Street. There were,
however, a limited number of places to go in French Ford;
you could go up Main Street to the railroad, you could
pursue Main Street in the other direction, to another part
of the railroad, you could go down to Deep Creek, you
could go to the diggings, or you could go to the graveyard.
We turned right, up the hill, onto Graveyard Road.

Graveyard Road would take us by the side lane that led
to the McCrackens' house. I said, "Maybe you don't want
to go by your folks' house."

"It's okay. I've been there already today. It was only
when my dad was alive . . ." His voice trailed off.

"You're a legend around here."

He seemed to take this seriously. "I thought about
French Ford. Lots."

"Evva and I used to talk about you. Even though *my* life
was happy. I mean, all the grown-ups were nice to me. But
I still thought about how you had run away. And Evva's
Dad was *mean* to her; she had her bags packed a couple of
times. We used to imagine you living in a hotel. And that
you had done something magical to the management so
they never noticed you were a kid; they just let you live
there."

David said, "I went into the diggings. I was there for
three weeks."

I said, oh. Maybe in the outside world living in the
diggings for three weeks would seem more romantic and
challenging than living in a hotel in Sacramento. But not to
anyone raised in French Ford. We were used to the diggings.

David and I had arrived at the side road that led to the

McCracken house. I stopped to look down at it. It was a clear example of what Daddy called Rural Squalor; he used to joke about that: "They lived in the little hamlet of Rural Squalor." The house leaned. It had an assortment of sagging gray porches; the roof was corrugated tin; frayed gray curtains belled lazily from one window; the other windows were curtainless. In the yard the yellow-white McCracken dogs lay in a star pattern; there was a stack of motorcycles, weeds, hubcaps. I looked at David to see if he was embarrassed. He was smiling.

"I used to miss it a lot. I used to dream about it."

I had always thought David ran away from home because he couldn't bear being a McCracken. Apparently not.

Maybe he read my expression. "It was my father. You've read those articles about how a parent will begin to hate one child? Just one of the children?"

"Yes."

"Well, I was it."

We had now started up the incline leading to the outer reaches of the graveyard. On either side was a continuous mat of dark green juniper punctuated by tilted, haphazard stones. To our right the vista of the town flickered between trees. I looked at our two sets of feet, David's in dark blue sneakers, mine in orange sandals. "I thought the child that happened to was damaged."

"Usually."

We scuffed for a minute or so more, and he said, "My mother was on my side. And my brothers. Ed says that's unusual. The family usually goes along with the parent who's being a tyrant. But my mother was *for* me. She had a strong personality."

"Who's Ed?"

He sounded surprised. "My foster father. The head of the Friends' Settlement in Fairfield. My mother got them to take me in."

Fairfield was a hundred miles south of French Ford, a small flat valley town below Sacramento. It wasn't as far away as San Francisco. But it seemed more distant. I had never known anybody in Fairfield.

We were now abreast of the graveyard entrance pillars, gray, with long spills of gray lichen on their inside surfaces. I tried to remember whether David's mother—her name, I thought, had been Sue Ann—was she buried here in this cemetery? She had been brown-haired and had had skeletal arms projecting from a print dress, dark-circled eyes watching in a creased face. I thought about her, living each day in that drama, hiding her child from his father. "Did she plan for you to run away?"

"Sure. She drilled me on it, how far into the diggings before I turned west; don't try to sleep in a cave; thrash the bushes before you lie down to sleep—there may be rattlesnakes."

"Not at night," I objected.

David said equably, "Well, *I* saw snakes at night. And she would come down there and bring me food. I was camped out in Dogtown."

Dogtown was a ghost town of five houses. It included the ruins of the Dogtown Bar.

"I used to dream about that afterwards," he said. "Sleeping in Dogtown. And waking up in the middle of the night, the crickets calling, the buildings creaking—the whole place is falling down, and me needing to go to the bathroom and not wanting to get up for it, looking at the

84

stars, wondering what was going to happen. And then seeing, across the diggings, this spot of light, knowing it was my mother, with a flashlight."

I thought some more about Mrs. McCracken, slipping out of the house for that late night journey. Maybe she was prepared to say, if Lyle McCracken caught her, that she was going to check on the dogs.

Sue Ann McCracken had had seams beside her eyes and at the corners of her mouth. But the big dark-ringed eyes were what you saw when you recalled her face.

"Why," asked Evva, "did you take him to the *grave-yard?*"

I wished now that I hadn't told Evva about my session in the graveyard with Steve. It had nothing to do with David McCracken.

"You could have gone into the diggings."

I didn't answer this. As a matter of fact, we *had* gone into the diggings. And I wasn't going to tell Evva about that.

It began as David and I walked down from the grave-yard. "There were a couple of things in French Ford I used to remember," he said, "One was the General Store. The way the inside is made of those blocks of stone and is dug into the side of the hill. And when you come inside the store it's dark and cool, and all that stuff is hanging from the rafters . . . The other thing I thought about was the Deep Sink. I would remember the Deep Sink when I was falling asleep. And then I'd come awake with a jolt, because I thought: what if, some fall, it dried up and never came back again?"

The Deep Sink was a pool in the diggings. It was situated, against all the laws of hydrodynamics, at the top of a hill. When you walked out to the Deep Sink you went uphill, across ruts and gullies, around manzanita bushes and dazzling rocks, until you thought that you, too, were turning into a baked white pebble. And then you crossed a rise and there it was, in shades of aquamarine and navy, its banks streaked white, with splashes of orange and purple. At the beginning of the summer the Deep Sink was about two hundred feet long. But the pool became smaller as the season wore on, until at the end of October it was only a mud puddle as big as our living room floor. That was the picture David had woken up with: what if, some year, the water never came back in the Deep Sink after its fall evaporation?

"It was all right two weeks ago," I said. "Do you want to go out there?"

David said yes, and we started along Main Street. I wondered briefly about stopping to get a bathing suit for me, one of Daddy's suits for David, a thermos of iced tea . . . and then abandoned this idea; it made the walk seem too much like a date.

It wasn't exactly true that I had never dated anybody but Steve. I had gone out a few times with the Colfax High School boys, and Neil Bailey from Becky Springs had taken me to the Senior Prom. But these dates had never gotten anyplace; my mind had been on other things. I believe I had the reputation among the boys of playing hard-to-get.

I wanted to ask David what he found to talk to his brothers about, but I didn't know how to phrase it.

"It's funny how you don't forget," he said, as we turned down Deep Creek Road.

86

We were silent for a while. Finally I asked, "How did you get your internship in the District Office?"

He looked down at me. There was surprise on his face. "Why, your cousin. Your cousin Steve. Your . . . fiancé?"

I opened my mouth to say, Steve, exclamation point, and then didn't say it. There were a lot of things Steve didn't tell me. "How did he know you?"

David sounded surprised some more. "Well, through my brothers. He and my brothers are friends."

Of course, of course. And you, Grace, are an unobservant, stupid dolt. And there goes your theory about how David McCracken is so far above his brothers that he never has anything to talk to them about.

David talks to his brothers about how they got him a job.

"I won't ever understand Steve." I hadn't expected to say this aloud. We were now walking away from the dark green Creek Road into the white diggings; the words echoed out against the bright diggings floor.

"Steve's hard to understand."

"Do you understand him?"

"Only some."

"I thought maybe another man . . ."

He shrugged. "Some people are just complicated."

David told me he was a student at Reed College in Oregon. He would go back there after six months in the Congressional District Office.

Now we were approaching the power pylons that stretched across the diggings, beginning at the left horizon and proceeding to the right one. The pylons were a series of spiky shapes joined by black cables. At the right horizon, on the crest of a hill, the king power pylon stood, its arms held wide and apart, a rope of cable attached to each wrist by a blue glass insulator. The pylons were clearly signalling somebody or something; alternately they were exclaiming or praying. Sometimes I thought they looked like praying mantises. (We didn't have praying mantises in French Ford, but I had seen pictures of them.) Sometimes they met my concept of what Martians should look like. If you stood under them their noise seemed to be inside you, a heavy mechanical buzzing.

We paused as we crossed under them. All French Ford children knew about stopping under the pylons and getting that thrill. The rumor was that if you stayed for ten minutes you would die of a heart attack.

Neither of us made any comment, but after we had started walking again David said, "Did you ever try it? Waiting there?"

"No."

"Argo once bet me ten dollars that I couldn't. And I couldn't. I started out and lasted six minutes. And then I left."

"Did Argo *have* ten dollars?"

"Probably not. But I thought he did, and that was what mattered."

"Evva did something like that to me," I remembered. "She *dared* me."

"Daring was bad."

"It was a special dare. A magic dare. Do you remember the formula?"

"A double dare with dibs on?"

"That's right. And when someone used that formula they were challenging your . . ." I fished for a word.

"Pride."

"Right. And I wanted to do it very much. But I couldn't."

David stopped walking. "Do you want to try now?"

"No, I don't."

We started up the hill again. A couple of times I reached out toward his hand. I was used to walking with Steve and holding hands. But both times I checked myself before I actually touched David.

After a few more feet he stopped walking. "Let's go back and do it."

We stared at each other. Finally we turned around and walked toward the pylons. David stationed himself under the uphill pylon wire and I stood under the downhill one; we faced each other. The nearest tower was about twenty feet away; it stood on a monolithic cement platform with an enamel label: Property of Pacific Gas and Electric. Above this cement base the pylon's pitted metal feet rose, the struts of a construct that ended somewhere out of sight in the moted blue sky.

David and I stood facing each other, surrounded by a circle of sound. It seemed clear that the sound made a circle, or maybe it was an oval, with one of its narrow ends above our heads and the other end buried under our feet. We stood in the middle of the oval, like those medieval saints that had a halo all the way around them.

Noise can be dangerous, I thought; the right note played on a cornet will shatter a pane of glass; there is a torture where they beam the same sound at you until you collapse. And ever after that you have dreams, awake and asleep, that you can't stop, and the echo of that sound is always pulsing inside you.

I looked up at David. The white diggings gravel reflected

glare into his face, gilding his chin and one of the cords of his neck. David was my age. I was used to Steve's face with the lines beside the mouth and the sag near the eyes. There was something threatening about David's smoothly textured skin, the sturdiness of the neck cord, the way the dark eyebrows arched toward each other, each hair springy.

I said, "Is it okay to talk?"

"I don't think so."

I practiced staring at our feet, but found myself, without wanting to, looking up again at David's face. A shadow crossed it, maybe the shadow of a bird; there weren't any clouds. The noise encased us; making a figure eight now, a loop around him, one around me, a knot in the middle. Without planning anything particular I took a step forward. David took one toward me. The noise had invaded my chest cavity; it filled up my breasts, especially the nipples; I thought of the nipples as turned out and up, absorbing something. I stared up at David: how smooth his face was; the cheekbones and neck cord glistening. He had a red mark where he had cut himself shaving; he had a few faint grains of beard.

I said, "I can't. We've got to stop."

He didn't argue. He stepped out from under the shadow of the wire and reached a hand toward me. I stretched one toward him. And then nothing happened; neither of us completed the gesture. We turned around and walked, side by side, or as much so as the rough ground would permit, up the hill.

Neither of us talked for a while. Finally David said, "I'd forgotten that the clay around here was purple." And he bent over and picked something up. And fooled with it for a minute, and then threw it off into the bushes.

At the Deep Sink we sat on the top of the rise, looking down toward the pool, which was jagged, very blue, and had a large gray driftwood spike, the remains of a buried tree, sticking out of the water at the far end.

Nobody said anything about swimming, although it was hot and we were both panting after our climb.

"Does it look the way it should?" I asked.

"Yeah. Just exactly."

I watched David's hand, resting on the edge of his pants, and enjoyed the fact that I didn't know anyone else who had fingers like that, with square-topped nails. All the Dowells had the same kind of hands, with oval fingertips.

David said, "It's funny about memory. I've been thinking about that poem: 'There was a man of double deed/ Who sowed his garden without seed . . .' "

David and I both knew this poem because it had been a favorite of Mrs. Georgeson, who taught third grade in the French Ford Elementary School. Now we went through it, reciting and prompting.

"It ends on a sinister note," David reminded. " 'And when his heart began to bleed/Then that was death, and death indeed.' "

"I'd forgotten the end." I was lying. I had been thinking about the ending the whole time. I had even written another couplet for the poem, and I remembered that, too:

> And when he wanted to recover
> Nobody could help him ever.

The whole poem was really about Steve. I had always understood that, ever since the first time I heard it. And furthermore, we were quoting it wrong. It really went: "And when *my* heart began to bleed/'Twas death, and death, and death indeed."

At the bottom of Main Street David said, "Well, I had better go get my bus."

I told him it had been a nice afternoon. "I liked talking to you."

Then I remembered there was something more, and I added, "Thank you for my ring."

11

"Hey, let's see the ring, baby." My father seized my hand. It was eleven at night; we were both in the kitchen. I was eating an apple; he was pouring a glass of California red; he had just gotten in from evening house calls. "Well, hold still, baby."

Our kitchen had twelve-foot plank ceilings and narrow-doored cupboards, so tall that none of us could remember what was on the upper shelves. "Wow," my father said, "that's gorgeous."

I said, "Daddy, what would you think if someone sent someone else up with the ring?"

This had to be explained more fully, of course. The explanation took a while. By the time I was through explaining my father had lost his hey-babe insouciance. "You know what they would say . . ." he started, his eyebrows down over his light eyes.

"Who's *they?*"

"In med school. There's a lot of psychiatry in med school these days. They'd say he was afraid."

I objected. "Of what? I'd already told him *yes*."

Daddy shook his head. I could see him moving away from his involvement in this, pretending to clear his ears as if he were coming up from under water. "Hey, not to worry, okay?" He drank; the rim of the glass clinked against his teeth.

When I insisted, "But Daddy. Afraid? Of me? Of emotion? Of dropping the ring and making a mess of it?" he shrugged. "Babycham. Steve's *original*."

Steve is weird. That was the way Evva put it.

Steve's response to my letter was to ask me to come to San Francisco. He said he could explain himself better in San Francisco. When we were face-to-face he would make me understand.

Look, darling Grace, this is a lot of hoopla about nothing, nada, zilch; it was just a sporadic impulse, for X sake, sort of mad sad wit; will you come to S. F., my darling, I want to show you my place and space all for my darling Grace . . .

Grace dear you are giving me bad dreams with ur questions what am I supposed to have done stolen the damn thing come to S. F.

The more Steve wanted me to come to San Francisco, the more reasons I found to postpone thinking about the idea. This was eccentric of me; I recognized that. I had been wanting to get out of French Ford; I had hardly traveled in all my life; what was the matter with me?

The trouble, Grace, is that you don't understand me, I mean the desperate chaotic me that crouches under a rock and has to be dragged out by its little protesting worm's head . . .

Oh, phooey.

I filled my pocket with quarters and went down Main Street to the telephone booth in front of the General Store. It was a white night with a big moon making the street pale in its dusty places; the moon gilded the front of the store, the three gas pumps, Young Utopia Hall. I sat down in the phone booth and propped *The Magic Mountain* on the ledge. With the combination of moonlight and the booth's fifteen-watt bulb I could just see to read.

I was calling Steve from the pay phone because this conversation might turn out to be peculiar and I didn't want Daddy hearing it. Also, I had waited for a time when Evva would be off the switchboard.

It took four tries to get Steve. One of the McCracken dogs appeared and lay down with its chin on the telephone booth ledge. I said, "Lucy," (that was tonight's operator), "try his number some more."

Lucy would listen in on my call, but she wouldn't listen in the same professional, ruthless way as Evva.

Finally Steve answered, and we had some preliminaries about how are you, and then more preliminaries about the ring: "Don't you like it?" "Yes, I like it." "Something's wrong with my taste?" "Your taste is fine."

"You don't take me seriously," I said. "You look at me. You don't see me."

Steve began to talk fast. "That's ridiculous, Grazia; you're crazy, I not think of you, my God, what do you mean?" His voice went down a notch; the consonants got hard. "I never loved you more, never." I supposed he meant than when he sent David along with the ring.

Lucy came on the line and said, three minutes.

Steve said, "Not care for you? You're batty." He sang, "I care for you/More than you dream I do . . .

"Listen," he said, "not care for you? I *dream* about you."

"I don't want to hear about the dreams."

"You have to hear about them. They're part of me. I dreamed you were in the middle of a big staircase. Your hands over your head. You held them that way yourself."

"Steve, you haven't listened to me; you never listen to me."

"Not listen? Why don't *you* listen? Grazia, you accuse me, you *accuse* me of the very thing you're doing; you've closed off your soul. You've got to hear about my dreams; they're *me*. This dream was in an underground hall; I don't know how I knew that; I just knew. And the underground hall had a temperature of . . ."

"Stop it."

"A temperature of absolute zero. You came down the stairs with your hands over your head . . ."

"Steve, are you drunk?"

"The light in the hall was blue, because of the cold; absolute zero; it must have hurt a lot. And now here is the part that I think about, Grace; it's strange; I don't know what it means; I've been thinking about it a lot. There was a metal picket fence at the bottom of the stairs. And sticking on one of the pickets of the fence there was this small animal, maybe a rabbit or a cat . . ."

I hung up the receiver. The McCracken dog came and put its head in my lap. The telephone swallowed quarters;

I sat with my head against the coin box. After a while the phone started ringing.

I let it ring seven times before I picked up the receiver. Lucy said, "Grace, Steve has been trying to get back to you."

"Grace. Grace, darling. Hello?"

"Yes."

"I'm sorry. But I want you to know. Everything."

"I don't *want* to know everything."

"How can you help me unless you do?"

"I can't help."

"You can. You're the only one who can."

After a while he said, "I need you. Maybe I can manage if I have *you*. Please. Come down here. I have to see you."

"I'm busy."

"Please come."

"I can't."

Steve said, "Grace, I'm worried about myself."

He said, "After I had that dream I couldn't sleep. I walked around my apartment and then I got dressed and went outside and walked and suddenly I was at the waterfront and I don't remember how I got there. I *need* you."

The dog burrowed its nose under my belt. I said, "I'll see if Evva can come with me," and hung up.

A minute later the phone rang again. Steve was calling to arrange where I would stay and what bus I would take. He sounded cheerful again. At the end of this conversation he said, "I sent David McCracken up with the ring to show you how much I love you."

I didn't answer this. But I was feeling slightly better.

"It was because I think we're royalty. That's what royalty does. The king doesn't deliver the ring himself; he

sends a second. Good night, dearest; good night, my darling."

This time Steve was the one who hung up. I sat for a
minute more cuddling the McCracken dog's ears. Then I
rose and started toward home.

Every now and then Indiana had shown me a page of her
diary, saying, "I thought you might want to look at it,
know what I mean?" and then had leaned over me to
watch me read, her blonde hair touching me on the shoulder. She seemed to draw sustenance from reading the page
along with me. "It's just kind of what I felt about" (that
snow we had last December) (the guys in front of the
General Store), she would say dismissively. But her writing
was unexpectedly good: circumstantial and eccentric. Although I had no forewarning of the way Indiana would
make us remember her later, I still noticed and recorded
bits of her diary in my memory.

Animals dead in the snow, she wrote, *curled up in the
foetal position* (three tries for the spelling of foetal), *not so
much frozen as dehydrated* (that one was spelled right),
*knees under the chin, were we always trying to go back
there, then, like a seed trying to be a seed again, tightening
so that nothing more can get in us, is that why Phil doesn't
like me to sleep like that and keeps waking me up when I
do?*

The Donner Party, Indiana said, *how the survivors had
curled up in the snow, dreamily, fatalistically; it was
hardly like anything at all, more like shifting your limbs,
adjusting your pillow before you fall asleep, and all part of
the natural process, look at coyotes, look at cats. Maybe
I'll go up to Donner some January and think about it.*

And the guys at the General Store, most people think they are undressing you when you go by, but that isn't how it is, more, they are dressing you: how would she look bare-breasted in my motorcycle vest? How would she look in my jock strap?

I dreamed last night that I was banging on the door of Grandmother's greenhouse. "Grandmother," I called out in passionate entreaty, "let me in, let me in . . ." Behind me was a wide field with factory smokestacks at the end of it . . .

Indiana's grandmother had been dead for seventeen years, and there had not been factory smokestacks near her greenhouse. Probably there weren't any factory smokestacks anywhere in Placer County.

Aunt Sybil told me today on Main Street: "Then I knew that someone had been there that wasn't right in their mind." After that she went into the General Store and stole herself a Popsicle.

There are a lot of people in our family, Indiana wrote, finishing that day's journal entry, *that are not right in their mind.*

12

Steve was excited to have us visit his office. He met Evva and me at the San Francisco Greyhound Bus Station and said, "Hello, darling," kissing me, cousinly, with closed lips. "Hello, Evva; come see my *place*."

"We want to go to our hotel."

"See my place first. Then your hotel."

Evva said, "Christ, Steve; I'm all sweaty." But Steve paid no attention to her. He pushed us toward a cab. "Embarcadero."

I had known that by his "place" Steve meant his office, But Evva seemed surprised. She had probably thought we were going to his apartment.

Steve put his arm around me. "Grace. Golden Grace."

"Don't mind me," Evva said.

"I'm not. Grace the fair. Beyond compare."

It was curious that Steve appeared to be making fun of me when he said things like this.

I stared at the white streets, at the white and pale blue

100

and pale pink houses, at the occasional vistas of water. "I lead a deprived life."

"A *deprived life*." Steve blew in my ear.

I was thinking that I had been to San Francisco only five times in my life. I went to Sacramento often, and that was all the traveling I had done. The porcelain chandelier in our dining room had been bought in Florence, the white leatherbound books in France; the Hogarth print over the fireplace came from England; the leather hassock from Morocco. My parents, aunts, uncles, and second cousins had gone to these exotic and educational places to buy these things. And I had not even gone to college. True, I had said I didn't want college. But why hadn't somebody insisted?

"Move over," I said to Steve. "I want to see."

"Me too," Evva said.

"I love you anyway." Steve seemed pleased to be showing us San Francisco.

He kept his arm around my shoulder and squeezed. He didn't mind when Evva said, "Oh, my God, Grace, that white steamer with the blue stack," although usually, when she and I showed a special understanding, he got jealous.

His District Office was on the second floor of a cement building, across the street from a line of docks. Between the pier buildings you could see slices of water and bits of ship.

"Here we are. Up you go, peerless, peerless Grace." He shoved and cajoled us up a steep flight of linoleum steps.

"Now then; how's that; my kingdom. Grace, you see it before you. Manifest. In all its glory . . . Hello, Wing."

He greeted a Chinese man wearing a pea jacket and a navy-blue knitted watch cap.

Steve's voice when he talked to me had been light, mocking, and high tenor. When he addressed the Chinese man his voice-pitch went down.

"What would you call it," he asked me, "neo-warehouse?"

Evva said, "You could sure use some paint."

Steve's District Office was high-ceilinged and gray, with steel struts holding up the roof. An enormous poster hung on the far wall: Jerry Shaughnessey made of gray dots, smiling and black-browed, intersected by a slogan: JERRY CARES. A red linoleum floor held islands of furniture, red leatherette chairs and couches, people hunched into coats. It looked like the Colfax gym on registration day except that the crowd was older and was half men and included a lot of Chinese people.

"Come on, you should meet the guys." The voice was that of the Steve who hung out at the gas pump with the McCrackens.

People were waiting, he explained, for their number to be called. They might be waiting to see the social worker, or to see him, Steve, or perhaps to see his secretary.

I looked around the office, Steve's place. I was trying to understand him, just the way he had asked me to. Here was where he operated. He complained about his office, but he liked it, too. People had been waiting for him here; everyone in the room had looked up when he came in, a mass head movement like the one you saw at a tennis match. Two men in sailor's jackets had gotten out of their chairs and come forward, saying things like, hey, Steve, or Steve, guess what?

The atmosphere was what I thought of as masculine; there was a big metal coffeepot, white china mugs, lots of cigarette butts, beer cans in the wastebasket. But there were women here too, and a baby, crying rhythmically. Steve paused on his way through the room to rub the baby's head; it stopped crying for a while.

Steve and the secretary had desks in a glass cage under the poster. I looked to see if the secretary had long red hair, and she didn't. She was Chinese. Also, I looked around for David McCracken, but he wasn't there.

Evva stretched out on the Mark Hopkins' peach-colored bedspread. There was a ruffle around the rim of the bed; by stretching her arms and legs she could touch both ends of it. "Steve is weird."

"He was nice today."

"He's weirder when he's nicer." After a pause she asked, "Why did you say we're sisters?"

The room clerk had asked if we were sisters, and I had agreed. Since we didn't look alike, it must have been our similar brown velvet hats that made him think of this.

And then I had had to change my story, because of our different last names.

It was no good trying to explain to Evva that the lie was connected with Steve and the District Office and the way he had spoken to me in the car.

"If you were going to say it," Evva told me, "you should have *stuck* with it. You could have been more inventive. You could have said we had different fathers. Or, one of us was married." She stretched some more. "I don't guess there's any chance Lloyd will take me to a place like this."

"Enjoy it while you're here." I was worried about some aspects of this visit.

Evva and I were supposed to buy my wedding dress. "No," Sybil had said, "you cannot let Evva make your dress and you cannot buy a dress at Weinstock's in Sacramento. There is only one thing you can do and that is to go to the fourth floor of I. Magnin's. The fourth floor of I. Magnin's is where we have always bought our dresses."

"Always?" I had asked.

"Always."

"It will take at least three days to buy this dress." Sybil had stood in the middle of Main Street and talked more to Evva than to me. "First, there is the fabric." "Yes," said Evva. "And then the line; line is important; she is so thin." Evva seemed to understand.

"The fit across the bust," Sybil had said; "yes," said Evva; "the spread of the skirt"; "yes"; and on and on while I stood beside them, feeling extra.

"She will look elegant," Sybil had summed up. "It will redeem the lustre that has been pulled from her wedding."

(Lustre. I pictured it as a coating like celluloid; you grabbed a corner and pulled, and off it came.)

"*Peau-de-soie,*" Evva had announced about the wedding dress material.

Evva asked now, from her place on the peach-colored bedspread, if I would have lunch with Steve.

No, I said, I would not have lunch with Steve; I would have dinner with Steve. That was to be the arrangement every night we were here. Dinner with Steve would be late. I would have early dinner with Evva and late dinner with Steve.

"Don't do *me* any favors," Evva said. "Who do you

think you are, Mrs. Good Deeds? Sometimes you act like you're IT: sometimes you act like you can fix up the whole world. Don't have dinner twice just to keep *me* company."

Evva liked to nag; I didn't pay any attention.

I was busy thinking about Steve and about going back to Steve's office and spying on him.

I was going to find out what was the matter with him. I would go down to his District Office some afternoon when he wasn't expecting me and sit contemplatively, invisibly in a corner, and watch. And find out.

Perhaps I would search his desk.

It never occurred to me that there wouldn't be a specific, identifiable something that was bothering him. I would find it out, *rout* it out was the way I thought of it.

I would save us both. I would save him; I would save me. Whatever it was, I would conquer it.

"What?" I said to Evva. "You don't want to eat early? We can eat later if that's what you want."

Evva said, "Oh, for Christ's sweet blessed sake," and turned on her side as if she were going to sleep. She looked pretty with her brown curls against the peach bedspread, and I went over to the bed and tickled her. "Come on," I said. "Come to dinner; we'll have cracked crab; I know about a place where they give you a bib with a picture of a crab on it." There was yet another thing that was bothering me; I certainly wasn't going to admit it to Evva, and could only obliquely state it to myself: why wasn't Steve inviting me to his apartment? At all? Evva wouldn't have cared; it would have been easy enough for him to do.

He wasn't able to see me that night until quarter of eleven. By the time he telephoned, Evva had gone to sleep

105

with her head under the pillow. I sat under the lamp, reading the first volume of *Remembrance of Things Past*. Steve had said that *Remembrance of Things Past* was the ultimate novel, but I missed *The Magic Mountain*. There are some books that one simply ought not to finish.

I met Steve downstairs and we went into the bar. He ordered drinks and a sandwich and sat staring at the mahogany panelling. Finally he picked up my hand and began to play with it; he traced the creases in the palm and turned the hand over, bent the fingers back, outlined four fingernails. He looked at the markings on my wrist and said, "That line is called the Girdle of Venus. If it's unbroken it means a woman is congenitally unfaithful."

I pulled the hand away. I'd be damned if I'd ask what was the matter.

But a minute later he volunteered. "All hell broke loose after you left this afternoon. Some psychotic had a fit. He lay on the floor and twitched. And there was a fight. Two of the warehousemen had a fight. I had to separate them."

"What about?"

"About who should see the social worker. They thought they both had the same number.

"And then Jerry called from Washington. Some citizens' committee is investigating his politics. He wants a lot of clergy endorsements."

"Can you get them?"

He shrugged. "Everybody's scared. God," he said. "I can't stand the stuff people complain about. It would be okay if they'd say, I'm hungry, I'm lonely, my kids are hungry, my wife hates me, life stinks. But no: yammer, yammer; the coffee's cold; she didn't say good morning, only hi; what does she think I am, dirt; he took my chair when he knows goddamn well it's *my* chair; what does *he* think I am . . . ?" Steve slammed his hand on the table and the glass ashtray jumped.

I didn't say, they talk about those things because they're afraid to think about the other stuff; probably Steve had figured this out for himself.

The waitress arrived with the drinks; Steve began to sip at his. "Oh, well, what the hell," he said. "Congress is getting idiotic, too. There is this half-wit named Mc-Carthy. Another Irish half-wit. Grace, the beautiful, talk about your sartorial plans."

"My what?"

"What kind of wedding dress you're going to buy."

"No."

"Why not?" He picked up my hand again and bent a finger back until I said ouch. Then he muttered, "Oh, my God, forgive," and lifted the hand and kissed it.

I said, "I'm sorry if it was a bad day," but he didn't want to talk about that any more. He was quiet for a while, and when he did talk it was about Sartre's *Nausea;* he was reading it for the second time.

After we had finished our drinks he took me upstairs and stood with me in front of my door and kissed me, tilting his head, holding the back of my neck, pressing himself against me. When we separated for a minute I said, "Why, Steve, why?" I wasn't as overcome as I usually was with him; I could hear Evva telling me *Steve is weird;* I could remember the metal picket fence from his dream. *Impotence,* the dictionary had said, *incapable of sexual intercourse. Said of males.* That didn't seem quite right. "Why, what?" Steve asked. "Why are we here at all? Why anything, why is life short; what are you asking, Grace, the

107

graceful?" And he reached around me, took the key out of my hand, unlocked the door, and pushed me through it, saying, "Good night, darling; sweet dreams."

The next day Evva and I stayed so long at I. Magnin's that I carried the store's air-conditioned, perfumed odor on my skin. "Some women do that all the time. They go shopping every day."

Evva said, "They can't," but without conviction. She was lying on the bed examining the seams of a blouse and making criticizing noises. "Look at that. The margin they allow. Only an eighth of an inch."

In the evening I called Daddy and Mrs. Farmer, and waited for Steve.

"What in hell is the matter with him?" Evva asked. "He's acting worse."

"He's been working hard."

"Does Steve take *drugs?*"

The television in the I. Magnin's ladies' room had showed a four-person discussion of drug addiction. "Don't be an idiot."

But I knew what she meant. The unfocussed green eyes, the quiver near the mouth, the twitching muscle under the chin. Evva said, "Is he worried about something?"

Steve and I went down to the bar. "I'm not worried about *anything.*"

He squeezed his martini glass and it snapped. The high clear noise echoed across the room. He and I stared at the sliver of glass reflecting the blue bar light, at the mess with the little bowl on its side, the olive rolling across the table. A black stain grew between Steve's thumb and forefinger. He wrapped his paper napkin around his hand.

"You may have sliced a tendon."

"No, I haven't." He turned the shard of martini stem. "Look at that, look at the way it catches the light." The shred of glass stood up, collecting glitter on its broken surface. "Maybe that's what I need."

"What?"

"Something sharp. Snapped short."

"Listen," I said, "where's David McCracken?"

"David? You mean Duke. Why in hell are we talking about Duke?"

"I thought he'd be at your District Office."

"Duke got sent to Washington for two weeks. The Congressman needed another peon." Steve captured the olive and mashed it around in the martini liquid. "*I* sent him to Washington for two weeks. I wanted to get rid of him."

"Get rid of him? Why?"

"You don't like him."

"I like him fine. It was the ring business I didn't like."

"Well, *I* don't like him." He squeezed the olive to make it squirt. "Sometimes I hate him."

When I didn't respond he said, "He's so goddamn clean. What business does he have being a McCracken and being so clean?"

We were silent for a while, and I said, "We'd better get the waitress to mop the table."

"Don't you dare." He held his hand protectively over the wet black plastic. "I like it this way."

In the elevator Steve took the napkin off and extended his hand.

I reached toward him, but he twisted away and said, "Look!"

We stood watching the line of blood that started between his thumb and first finger, ran down his thumb, dripped off the end of the nail onto the beige elevator floor. "See? See that?"

I could feel him staring at me; I knew the look, the one where the black eye-centers got small and tight. I said, "Goddamn it, Steve, cut it out."

He laughed, brushed the hair out of his eyes, and grasped my arm; when he let go he left a speckled handprint and a long drip down the inside forearm.

"I've marked you. You're mine; I've marked you." He bent down and kissed me on the bloody place.

13

On Thursday Evva went home. I rode down to the Grey-hound Bus Station to see her off.

"It was swell," she told me. "Thank your dad for me."

"Listen, I'll pay you back," she said. "You'll see. What's the best hotel in Paris? I'll take you to the best hotel in Paris. When we're thirty-five."

We decided the best hotel in Paris was the Crillon.

"Evva?"

"Yes?"

"Go see Sybil?"

Evva said, sure, without her usual lecture about Sybil being crazy.

"Listen," she said, with one foot up on the bus step, "do you know what it is . . . that makes Steve . . . that makes him not take you home to his apartment?"

"No."

"He's afraid of you."

"No, he isn't."

"He is. I've watched him. Not afraid, like, you were

dangerous, but still. When he calls you all those Spanish names."

"Italian."

"That's because he's afraid. He's scared to look at you and call you Grace."

The bus driver leaned out over the step and told us, "Hey, ladies, break it up; how about let's get this thing airborne." Evva kissed me. "I read it in my psychiatry book; some men, if they think a woman is good, they're afraid of her. And if they don't think that, they're not. They're only afraid of the good ones."

I said, "Good" and made a raspberry. She kissed me again, in a gingerly manner; we weren't usually demonstrative.

She looked very handsome climbing up the bus step in her brown suit and close-fitting hat made of brown velvet petals.

That afternoon I went down to Jerry Shaughnessey's District Office.

Sue, the secretary, said, "Hi." She had a thin, prowed face like the ones in Daddy's Aztec bas-reliefs.

"Steve meeting you?" she asked.

I said I was going to wait for him, and went to sit in the farthest red leatherette chair with a view of the bay.

I sat for an hour while Sue typed and clanged, answered the phone, exclaimed, "Oh, helldamn," all one word, called, "Be good," to departing friends.

The social worker closed her partition; the office boy washed the coffee cups. Sue put the cover on her typewriter. "Listen," she said from the door, "take my word for it. Don't let Steve make you wait like this, okay?"

Sue wore a red scarf and looked pretty, I thought.

I read *Newsweek*. There was a long article about bally girls. A bally girl is the one who stands outside a sideshow while the barker makes his spiel. She doesn't do anything, just smiles and tries not to look too cold. The one in the photo wore a gauze skirt and sequinned bra.

The sky grew dark, the water changed from blue to gunmetal, a squadron of triangular sailboats passed, a small round fog cloud rolled by, turning like a tennis ball. Finally I heard Steve's step on the stairs.

He came into the room fast. I pulled back in my chair and he didn't notice me.

I watched him as he walked around, touching things. He clicked the top of an ashtray to make it swallow its cigarette butts. He straightened magazines, picked up a couch cushion by its corner and thumped it. I kept waiting for him to see me, but he didn't. Finally he went into the cage, turned on the light, and sat in his chair and drummed his fingernails on the space bar of his typewriter.

I tried to figure out what he would look like to an impartial observer. Like someone with a secret, his shoulders hunched protectively over his chest, his elbows moving minimally.

He opened a drawer and took something out and read for a while, some book, I heard him turning pages. Then he said "Jesus." Then he put his head down on the desk. He stayed that way for a minute. Finally he sat up, closed the drawer, and turned off the light.

I had been considering telling him I was here. Now I didn't want to do that. What I wanted to do was wait until he had gone, until I heard his footsteps receding down the staircase.

Then I would get up and go in the cage and search his desk.

Steve's middle drawer held neatly organized pens, pencils, erasers, paper clips, evidence of the organized Steve rather than the chaotic one. The top left-hand drawer had stationery, the next one a dictionary. The third drawer stuck as if it were supposed to be locked; finally it popped open. It contained only one object, dead center, instantly recognizable with its block-printed Japanese cover and blue silk spine: Indiana's diary.

The cover was watermarked, as if someone had spilled tea on it, and there was something scrawled, in printing; it's hard to be sure with printing, but it looked like Indiana's.

Goodbye. That was what was written across the cover, diagonally, in smudgy print. Messy, the kind you would make with your finger, if you had dipped your finger in

. . .

I didn't want to think about this part of it. The color of the writing was the color of blood, dried blood. Indiana had dipped her finger in blood and written goodbye across her diary, and then she had sent it to Steve in the mail. Or else she had made a date with him and handed it to him, wearing a bandage around her wrist, blood beginning to seep through the bandage in a round bright stain; not just a token; suicides always try several times; don't pretend a suicide attempt doesn't mean anything; it's always a cry for help; it always means *stop me*, please stop me.

Steve with his assessing green eyes had watched her.

Grace, you are dramatizing; Evva is right; everything is a big stage-play, with yourself at the center.

114

Halfway down the stairs I began to cry. I didn't know why I was crying; there was no will involved; it just happened. I was going down the stairs holding onto the banister rail with one hand and I slipped. My knees gave way; my feet didn't focus properly. I sat and put my head between my knees. After a while I touched my cheek and it was wet, as wet as if I had been in the shower.

Where was I supposed to go now? Not to the Mark Hopkins; Steve would be coming there. Maybe I could walk to French Ford. French Ford was a hundred forty miles away; if I walked five miles an hour I would be in French Ford in a day and a half.

But I couldn't go to French Ford. French Ford had been ruined. I could never see Daddy, nor Sybil, nor Mrs. Farmer again. All of us were involved in this crime.

I didn't know what the crime was, but Evva was not in it. She was home free.

I got up off the stairs. I was still dizzy, but not too bad. And finally I walked to the Mark Hopkins by way of Fisherman's Wharf. It took me two hours.

Steve followed me across the hotel lobby. "Where in *hell* have you been?"

Then he must have looked more closely. "What is it? Are you hurt?"

I looked at him.

"What is it? Grace? My God, tell me." He put his hands on my shoulders. "Wait. We'll get to the room. You'll tell me."

He got the room key away and struggled to unlock the door. I thought, He thinks I've been raped. *Good.*

He turned on the lights and pushed me toward a chair.

115

His hands were shaking. (*Good.*) "What happened? What did someone do to you?"

"It's you. Not someone. You."

"Oh." He said this the way you say, *maybe I understand*.

"Indiana's diary says 'Goodbye' across its cover."

He got up and went to the window. The sky was quite dark by now. "You searched my desk."

"Yes."

"What right had you?"

I didn't answer.

"You're accusing me . . ." Steve said. "You're charging me . . ."

At this point all the lights in San Francisco went out.

They seemed to go out first in the hotel room and then in the city, but obviously this couldn't have been true. It was a minute before I could see shapes—Steve at the window, San Francisco behind him, the sky with a quarter moon.

Steve said, "Oh God." My eyes got more adjusted: a spectral line of glimmer under the eaves of the building across the street where pigeon droppings shone white against stone; a line of lights near the waterfront; an illuminated dome off to the right. Steve moved back to his chair, sat down, sighed, crossed and uncrossed his legs. A siren sounded.

We were silent; it seemed impossible to talk in the dark. Finally there was a knock on the door and the bellboy entered, pushing a cart with a kerosene lantern on its prow. "Boy," he said, "some blackout." He handed us candles in metal holders, matches. "Boy," he said, "nobody knows anything."

Steve set one candle on the coffee table and another on

the lamp stand. The room came slowly back into focus. His face flickered and flared.

He sat back down. "Okay. Let's get this over."

"I've changed my mind."

"What do you mean, changed your mind?"

"I don't *want* to talk."

"Well, I *do*."

"I won't listen."

"You started this."

I put my hands over my ears.

He said, "Don't think I'm excusing myself."

I kept my hands in position.

"Don't think I'm offering reasons . . ."

His voice came through my cupped hands. "Indiana came to my place . . . It was about one in the morning."

Finally I just let him tell me.

"Indiana came to my room . . ."

"Where?"

"In San Francisco. My room in San Francisco. She knocked on the window . . ."

"On the *window?*"

"It's first floor. And when I opened it, she said . . . 'Grandmother, Grandmother, let me . . .' "

"Stop it."

We were silent for a while. The candle flame dimmed and strengthened. Another siren sounded. Steve got up and stood over the flame. Lighted from below, his face looked like an apparition in a séance.

He went on, "She said, 'Steve, I'm going to kill myself.' "

"She *told* you?"

"Yes."

"And then what? What after?"

"Nothing. She stared. You know how her eyes got. Sort of extra-focussed. The pupils got small."

(Like yours. Do mine do that?) "And what did you do?"

"I said, 'Come around to the side, Indiana. Let's sit down like civilized people. Let's talk.' "

Steve bent over the candle. It brightened his chin, his mouth with the drooping lines beside it, his pale hair. He looked celestial, like our glass Jesus. "That was great," he said, "that was very considerate and thoughtful. 'Come in, Indiana, let's talk' . . . Her teeth were chattering."

I thought about it. Indiana's teeth were chattering. And then Steve ushered her into his first-floor apartment and sat her on a chair. She was upright in the chair, shaking, her arms around her knees, thumbs hooked to control the shaking.

"And so you talked to her."

"I suppose you could say so."

"You tried to calm her down."

"Not exactly."

"You tried to get her to relax."

"No."

"You did something."

"I did nothing," Steve said in an uninflected voice. "Nothing is the exact word, the word that applies . . . I talked, in an interested, modulated voice, about the people in my office. I told her about who had come in. What letters I had answered.

"Do you want to know what I said to her when she asked me . . ."

I could see it approaching. "I don't want to know."

"When she said, 'Steve, Steve' (she was stammering, remember; her teeth were chattering and she was stammering . . .)"

"I don't want to know."

"She said, 'I can go, I think; I can go away quietly, not keep pushing it all the time, not keep hassling it; I'll get over it; I think I will. How will I manage without you? Yes, I will; I'll manage without you.'

"She said, 'Sometimes I hear it pretty clearly. That I can manage.' "

"Don't."

"It was the word *hear* that did it to me. She meant to say *know* and she said *hear* instead. Sometimes I *hear* it clearly. She mixed up her words just like a crazy Dowell. I was tired; I'd been up all night the night before; I'd been waked up. I wanted her out of my way, out of my chair. I wanted to wipe them out, all the Dowells in history, with their vague green eyes.

"She said, 'Just tell me I mean something to you.'

"I said, 'You mean nothing to me, Indiana. Really, nothing.' "

"You said that. You said, 'Nothing.' "

"That's what I said." Steve stared at me, eyes narrowed. I let out my breath. "So *you* did it. You killed her."

He moved his shoulders. " 'If the red slayer thinks he slays . . .' "

"Shut up. *Shut* up."

It was hard to read his face by candlelight; maybe the expression was contempt, maybe something else, like surprise. His tone continued light. "You haven't heard it all."

All? There's more? I didn't say this.

"There was a question that Indiana raised. It wasn't ever settled. The Placer County coroner isn't that thorough."

119

The coroner isn't that thorough. This was a line from a play. I thought I knew what was coming next. Oh, my God.

"Steve, *when* did she do it? How long afterwards did she do it? Kill herself?" Perhaps by asking this question I could change the direction this conversation was going.

"She killed herself the next afternoon."

My chair had wooden arms carved in a ridge pattern. I dug my fingers into them.

"There was an added question," Steve went on inflexibly, his voice monotone, his profile outlined by window light. "Indiana got ideas; maybe she was wrong. But she thought she was pregnant."

I leaned forward, grabbed the chair arms, and pulled my knees up to my chest. I was waiting to be sick. A set of luminous traveling spots, like gnats, grew in the candle halo. They circled the flame; my ears filled with sound. Dimly, out of the side of my vision, I saw Steve stand up and wait by the candle; finally he reached out and snuffed it. "So now you know. Everything about me."

I expelled a breath. I wasn't going to be sick after all.

"Do you hate me?" he asked.

"Yes."

He moved toward the door. "That philosopher who talked about betraying your best friend . . .

"It wasn't a philosopher; it was a writer. And the thing you do, the act; you know what it's called?

"It's called the *acte gratuit,* the gratuitous act. It has no particular point. It's not for revenge."

Afterwards I thought, had Steve been a radio program that I tuned into just then, I would have said his voice sounded thoughtful, considering. "I suppose it's just a gesture of despair. That's all. A gesture of despair."

When he was gone I started to pack. I didn't know where I was going. To some place away, far beyond my old life, not to French Ford.

I kept throwing stuff into my suitcase and telling myself, now, Grace, you are beginning to understand; Grace, now maybe you're starting to understand.

14

"Hi," said the bus driver. "Going back to Dry Gulch? Going to tell them about the big city?"

It was the same driver Evva and I had had. "It's French Ford," I told him, "not Dry Gulch. Did you make Dry Gulch up?"

"Uh-uh. I read it in a book."

I handed him my ticket. "I'm going to Reno."

He said some things about getting a divorce, and what had I done with my cute friend, and I said, ha-ha, yes, and moved to the back of the bus where I wouldn't have to talk to him any more.

Most of the ride until just before French Ford would be boring, at least from the standpoint of scenery. I watched my fellow passengers get on, and tried to think about them and who they were and what they did, but I couldn't get involved in these questions, the kind that usually appealed to me. Then I thought about literature and about how Myrtle in *The Great Gatsby* rode the train into New York telling herself: You only live once; you only live once. And then I thought about the man of double deed; and that was death and death indeed, and about this bus being almost full now, and if the side-by-side busload of people, arbitrary patterns for this ride, if they and their bus went off the road and everyone on the bus were killed, would we be partners then throughout eternity, go into the next world labeled "the busload to Reno," and I not allowed to see Sybil, or Daddy, or Mrs. Farmer or Evva, ever again?

I thought some about the next life, and got nowhere. The Dowells were not religious, unless you counted Jesus and the miners as religion.

I had been awake all night. This was the first time in my life I had done that. All night long, first with a lot of walking around, adrenaline so high I could have fueled a rocket to the moon with it. I stood at the window and stared out at the rekindled lights of San Francisco, then walked back and forth, fast, thinking, God, I'm going to blow up, right through the roof of the Mark Hopkins.

About two a.m. I called Evva's switchboard. But it wasn't her turn for night shift, so I hung up and lay down on the peach-colored counterpane. And when it was beginning to be light I started to pack. And had my suitcase half-loaded before I remembered that Reno was the place to go if you want to get lost.

The most difficult moment of the bus ride was the place on the highway where the Greyhound made its French Ford stop.

The driver pulled up there and the bus gave its snort-exhaust-fart. The driver climbed off his seat and walked down the aisle. "Hey, Blondie, you *rilly* not getting off?"

There was something about me—maybe it was my excessive Dowell pallor—that made me look younger than I was, so that strangers patronized me this way. "No, I'm not."

I rejected saying, I'm going to see an aunt in Reno, considered, I have a job in Reno, rejected that, too. I stared at the driver and pulled a question across my face: Why are you paying me this attention? It's none of your business.

"Okay, baby," he said, still looking troubled. He got off the bus and went off behind a tree—to pee, I supposed— while I sat and stared out at the familiar dark green pines and behind them the dark blue sky. I imagined what Sybil would be doing at this moment. She would be sitting rocking in her lawn chair, her eyes on the white diggings horizon. Or perhaps she was in the store, thinking what she would steal today. Maybe she was even buying something. Sybil did occasionally buy things.

I thought some more about French Ford, and stopped doing that when I got to our back porch with its yellow walls and blue-painted roof.

Then I pulled a pencil and souvenir menu from the Mark Hopkins out of my purse and began to write in the margin a poem about being a ghost in French Ford and wandering invisibly up Main Street. The bus driver got back on the bus; he noticed me writing and called out, "Hey, sending the folks a card, huh?"

He seemed reassured by this idea and turned his attention to the brunette behind him. They talked while she fed him sandwiches out of her blue hatbox.

When we entered Truckee I leaned my head against the window and started to cry. I felt hollow. I had felt that way when Sybil told me about Daddy's heart attack; when I described my feelings she had said, "Hollow. What do you mean, hollow?" and stared at me lopsided; you never knew beforehand what Sybil would understand and what she wouldn't.

The woman next to me was reading a green book and didn't pay any attention to my crying. I accomplished it silently; maybe she didn't notice.

Truckee was bare and windy and made of corrugated tin. At the Truckee bus station I got off the bus and went to the ladies' room. The lady with the green book preceded me; she stood in front of me in the line for a cubicle; she didn't say anything until she was the first in the line of waiting women; then she turned around and said; "Listen, hon, it's worst at the beginning and at the end." I wasn't sure whether she was talking about the restroom line or about life; maybe both. I decided I should be touched for having been noticed. She wore a tan polyester pantsuit.

An hour outside Truckee the bus crossed the border into Nevada and the scenery changed. I dislodged my head from the window and stared at the gray roadside ground and stunted trees and thought, well, different is new and thus better. I still had the Mark Hopkins menu open on my lap and wrote along one border, *And when the sky began to crack, it was a roof to break his back.*

The rest of the highway into Reno was downhill except for a space of twenty miles that was slashed by valleys with farms at their bottoms. We drove through this for a while, and then we entered Reno, which was flat and gray, with a background of mountains. I climbed down off the bus seat. The woman in the polyester pantsuit was in front of me again. She turned around and said, "Chin up, dear," so I knew it was my crying she'd been talking about before. I told her thank you and took my suitcase down the steps while I tried to collect my thoughts.

I had that phrase from Sybil, who would say, sitting in the diggings, the sun beating down on her straw hat, "No, I'm not going to have a stroke; no, this sun isn't too hot; I don't care what happened to the mother in *Return of the Native,* I am not going to die of heat prostration; I'm collecting my thoughts."

And finally it came to me; my thought.

I was in Reno where I could lose myself, and Reno had several permanent carnivals. Both Evva and Mrs. Farmer had told me so.

A carnival had bally girls. And being a bally girl was the only job I had heard of recently that I was perfectly certain I could do.

I would go check into the Hotel Reno, where Mrs. Farmer stayed when she came to Reno. (Apparently Christian Scientists were allowed to gamble, gambling was what Mrs. Farmer went to Reno for.) I had enough money for only two days at the Hotel Reno, so tomorrow I would go out to the carnivals and ask about a job as a bally girl.

I wondered whether you looked for carnivals in the Classified Section of the telephone book, and then decided that you didn't. I would ask the bellboy in the hotel.

Henry's Permanent Fun Show occupied a gray wooden building that contained the Game-a-thon, Madame Astarte, Palmist, Duchess Escort Service, the Dreamtown Ballroom, Salvatore's Human Oddities, and Intelligent Creatures.

Jerry the bellboy had warned me against Duchess and Dreamtown. They were, he said, "purely hoor operations," and he didn't think I wanted to . . .

"No," I said.

He also warned me against Henry's; it was the crummi-
est of the carnivals; it hadn't been painted for four years;
Henry usually couldn't afford a girl, but he just might . . .
Jerry stared at me sadly. He was incongruously tall and
had damp gray eyes. "Think you can hold him off?"

"Who, Henry?"

"Yeah."

"What'll he do?"

Jerry chewed on a rubber band. "He's not a judo spe-
cialist."

"I can manage it then."

Jerry refused a tip. "I feel bad about this. You're just his
type. He likes them skinny."

I wasn't worried about Henry. I was in a mood I had
read about, where you just don't care. At four-thirty that
morning I had stuck my head out the hotel window. The
street below was the one you have seen pictures of,
with a sign across it: RENO, BIGGEST LITTLE CITY IN THE
WORLD. It was first daylight, and the street was already
crowded; people milled slowly up one sidewalk and down
the other one, their feet obscured by a haze of dust particles struck golden by early sunlight coming between the
buildings.

I thought about Indiana and wondered if she were
around somewhere watching. Indy was purely generous;
she would feel sorry for me and not jealous because Steve
had once loved me, whatever he thought love meant.

Every three or four minutes the noise on the street inten-
sified; I finally figured out that this happened when the
door of the nightclub across the way opened and closed,
letting out a wave of saxophone music.

Finally I shut the window and went to take a bath. Then

127

I put on a pink linen-weave dress that made me look especially blonde, and after a while it was time to go down to breakfast.

I bought the *Reno Observer,* which had a story that mentioned Jerry Shaughnessey. "Bright, emphatic, a fighter," it said, "but can he outwit the House Un-American Committee?" I thought about this while I drank ice water and waited to order. Every booth in the coffee shop had a fruit machine so you could gamble while you were eating your pancakes.

And finally it was time to go in search of Henry's Permanent Fun Show.

Henry was in an office beside the ticket booth; the door was half open, he had his feet up on the wooden desk and was reading a newspaper.

"Well, good morning, Sunshine," he said, He was bald and lumpy, with a creased forehead.

He looked me over carefully and I could tell that if there was a job I would get it. He examined me the way Indiana had said the men on Main Street did, as if they were imagining the women wearing some special article of intimate male apparel. "Do you dance?"

"No."

"Juggle?"

"No."

He sighed. "Would you wear a padded bra?"

I couldn't see any reason not to wear a padded bra. "Yes."

He sighed some more."Be here at four."

"Hey," he added as I turned to go. "I *like* flat boobs myself."

At four o'clock Henry had changed the appearance of the Fun Show with a plywood sign and a spangled blue net curtain. He himself looked different; he wore black pants, a doctor's white smock, and an eye examination mirror on his forehead. He handed me a hanger with some blue net dangling from it. "Here, sugarplum fairy, climb into this."

In spite of the article in *Newsweek* magazine, I had only a dim idea of what a bally girl did. When I had my blue net costume on—it made me look busty and small-waisted, with the legs cut high on the sides—I sat on a stepladder and listened to Henry's instructions. The blue net costume had blue net stockings to match it; I fiddled with these to get the seams straight. "Now, you want to look mysterious, kind of, the point is not to look at any of these konks; eye contact is not good; with eye contact you'll maybe get one of them climbing up here to rape you, which is *not* what we want."

"What the hell." He seemed somewhat more nervous than I was. "It's all a bunch of crap, me, wearing this damn ophthalmology eye doctor thing; how do you like my sign?"

The sign, in uncompromising blues and greens, showed a jungle, water, prehistoric ferns, a crocodile, a snake, a naked woman, and the legend: HENRY'S FUN SHOW, MARVELS OF SEXUAL EXPERIMENTATION. I said that I liked the sign and Henry reminisced about how his ex-wife had gotten a talented thin man to paint it. "Skeleton Sam, he was really good; if he ever gained weight and lost his gig he could have made it as a painter."

By five o'clock three or four people had collected on the pavement near the sign, most of them with their backs to it as if they were not interested. Henry looked at his watch and said, "Okay, let's roll."

He dragged the stepladder platform out onto the pavement. "Now then, Starbright, up you go."

Then without any preamble he began, "Hey, ladies and gentlemen, ladies and gentlemen, speaking of our marvels of sexual experimentation." To my surprise a crowd formed right away; people must have been waiting all up and down the block, retreated into doorways. And in a few minutes Henry was admitting his first group of twelve saying, "And a dollar from this handsome gentleman and a dollar from this lady with the orchid in her buttonhole . . ." The lady's orchid was really a streaked and browning camellia; that was typical of Henry's approach to things.

Each day that week when I stood out in front of the Fun Show in my blue net costume Henry said, "Jeez, girl, you look great, I mean, *great,* how about it, honey, you know, come home with me tonight, everybody in carney does it, means no more than a handshake; Christ, don't know what you're missing until you've tried it."

And each day I told him that I was a virgin and he said, "Oh, Jesus Christ, okay, *okay,* so you're a goddamn virgin," and then he wouldn't say anything more about that for the rest of that day.

Except for this pass that he made every afternoon, Henry was not hard to work for. He taught me to move some while he made his spiel. I was supposed to turn slowly, staring at a corner of the Fun Show sign as if I could see my reflection there, and then turn some more and touch my hair and my hips. Henry approved of the way I did this and said it was seductive and that I had beautiful hair.

He was self-conscious about his baldness. "You know, doncha, that's a sign of a real good lover, that baldness, but of course *you're* not interested."

It took him about ten minutes to make a spiel; anybody that paused got included in the come-on. "Some of the seven wonders of the world, ladies and gentlemen, as thousands of intelligent people are perfectly willing to attest . . . This gentleman here, the one in the dark blue suit, this gentleman that is standing and staring so earnestly and scrutinizingly at our offerings, that's the clientele we have coming to view our wonders of sexual experimentation."

In between spiels Henry and I sat in his office or on the steps behind the Fun Show sign. He talked about his wife, who had left him to marry a certified public accountant, and about money, and the Fun Show, and how life was a gamble. I asked him questions about the wife because I was interested in people who used to be in love with other people. He said I was sensitive and intelligent. He said, "Jeez, kid, maybe I could really fall for you.

"But no," he added, "uh-uh, nope. No way. You are far, far above me." I had told him something about myself and that I was running away from someone.

"Why you got to run?"

"I don't know."

Henry was smoking a cigar. "He beat you, kid?"

"No. He did . . . a kind of crime."

Henry, thinking aloud, decided the crime had been petty larceny and that my boyfriend was a certified public accountant. "But I still don't get it about running away. A woman is supposed to stand by her man."

"He scares me. He can make me do anything."

"Ahhh." This tied in with some aspect of Henry's experience. "Gotcha." We sat moodily staring at the back of the Fun Show's sign. Sitting there was companionable.

I was living with Mrs. Rose now, on Wasatch Street. I had one room and kitchen privileges. Every night on my way home I tried to call Evva from the pay phone on the corner. Finally, a week and a half after I had arrived in Reno, I got her.

"My God," she said. "Jesus H. Christ."

I said, "Listen, Evva, will you call me back?" and gave her the number.

The switchboard must have been busy that night; it was a while before the pay phone rang. By the time it did I was crying. I said, "Evva, I can't come back to French Ford."

"What do you *mean?*"

"I can't come back. Not ever."

"You're crazy."

"Steve murdered Indiana."

There was a pause. Evva said, "Grace, you *are* crazy."

"No, he did." I blew my nose and started talking. It felt good; it felt like dropping a sackful of rocks. I got to *nothing, Indiana, nothing,* and Evva said, "Jesus." Then she said, "Oh, Jesus." Then she said, "Hold on a minute, my board is all lit up."

When she came back on it was, "Oh, my God, you poor kid." And then, "But Grace. I don't see what good staying away will do."

"Steve can make me do anything."

"No, he can't."

I didn't answer this, and Evva sighed. "Listen, for God's sake . . ."

There was more clicking as she fitted pegs into holes. When she came back on again she said, "Grace."

"I'm still here."

"I'll send you some money."

I started to cry some more, and we had an argument where Evva said yes and I said no, and then I told her about Henry's Fun Show, making it sound better than it was, with my pay twenty cents an hour higher and Henry funnier than he was, and we laughed, and Evva said, "Grace, this is dumb. You can manage Steve. I'll help."

"Evva," I told her, "I still love him," and then I began to cry really hard and Evva said, "Hey, there," and "There, there," and "Grace. Hey, Grace. It's *me*." She sounded as if she were crying too, which was unusual for her.

Before we hung up we had agreed that I would write to Daddy in care of Evva and she would pretend the letter came from Sacramento.

She said, "I'll come up to see you," and I said, "Don't," and she said, "Why?" and I said, "Maybe later," and then I hung up and sat with my hands in my lap.

Mrs. Rose's street was a quiet flat one with mountains at the end of it. Nobody was out late on Wasatch Street and there weren't any noises; it was October and the weather had become too cold for crickets. I walked slowly toward the house, a gray one covered in asbestos shingles. My room was in the back, off the wetmop porch.

The good thing about that was that I could come in late and not wake people. I had told Mrs. Rose I was an usher in a movie house.

I let myself in the back door and sat on the edge of the bed and thought about the fact that Evva had made me homesick and that I hadn't explained about Steve and hadn't told her the worst part of the story; maybe I would never tell that to anybody. In school we had read a novel about a woman who tied herself to the bedstead so as not to go down and meet her lover. And also there was Jane Eyre, who ran away from Rochester; I had never been able to explain that one to Evva, either.

15

There was not very much to do in Reno unless you gambled or drank, and I didn't do either. (Vodka with Evva didn't count, that was for French Ford.) And it was amazing how much working from four in the afternoon until one in the morning scrambled your life. It did this in Reno less than in most places, because in Reno you could have dinner or a drugstore Coke or a shopping spree in Woolworth's or a stroll down a crowded pavement anytime during the twenty-four hours. I tried all these things, Woolworth's especially. But Woolworth's was depressing at two a.m.; the fluorescent lights blinked chaotically; the jukebox stuck itself at "Doggie in the Window," and all the people were stealing things. At the hair-goods counter a woman stuffed a pink hairnet envelope into her purse. I was embarrassed for her; was I supposed to do something about this, tell the manager? So I moved away, and as I passed Flashlights another woman, a much older one, was counting batteries and dropping them in her coat pocket.

Maybe I was imagining it; maybe I missed Sybil so much that I had invented a Reno full of Sybils.

Sometimes at two a.m. I went to Stanley's Casino. Stanley's was the biggest casino in Reno; it was in a new building with a front like the prow of a ship. The angled glass sides stuck out over the sidewalk and people had to walk around them; behind the smoked glass windows colored shapes moved as if under water. The ladies in bobby socks and curlers who played the machines looked romantic and evocative when you saw them dimly through Stanley's front window.

Inside, Stanley's was not romantic, except for the Indigo Room, where the high money games were played on blue, not green, tables. Spectators weren't permitted in the Indigo Room, but the people who had been playing there came out to the metal and glass bar in the hall, and if I sat at this bar with a Coke I could listen to these people and invent stories about them. Some of the people were glamorous and thin and wore white sequinned evening dresses or black tuxedos; some looked like Henry; some were the curlered ladies from the front who had won enough on the bandits to play baccarat for the rest of the night. I eavesdropped on the white-sequinned ones, but most of them were too drunk to make stories out of.

The drawback about sitting in Stanley's back bar was that after ten minutes someone always tried to pick me up. I told these people that I was waiting for a friend, that I was meeting my husband, that my boyfriend was in the men's room. "Say you're a Reno policewoman," the bartender advised. He was nice, with dark bags under his eyes. He drank steadily and was too standing-up drunk to make passes at me.

I had two research projects. The first was to read Proust's *Remembrance of Things Past*. (I debated about this because of its association with Steve, but decided to do it anyway.) And the second project, a related one, was to find out about the House Un-American Activities Committee. If Jerry Shaughnessey was supposed to outwit the House Un-American Activities Committee, Steve, who was his assistant, would be working on that, too. Outwitting was one of Steve's big interests.

I asked Henry, "What *is* the House Un-American Activities Committee?"

"Are you kidding?"

I stuck my copy of *Newsweek* under the bally platform. "I don't understand this stuff."

"Listen, babychild, you're not supposed to *understand* it . . ."

It was cold on the street. Blue shadows edged the windy sides of the white buildings. Henry leaned against the bally platform and lit his cigar. "This bother you?"

"No." Henry liked to think he treated me like a lady.

"The House Un-American Committee," he said, "is this committee thinks everybody's a Communist."

"Why do they think that?"

"They don't think it; they say it. To get their name in the papers." Henry sighed. "You sure are innocent. Where you been living—in a seashell at the seashore?"

Henry knew where I had been living. "I don't usually read the newspapers."

"And they don't got any newspapers in French Bore?"

He sounded so cross that I decided not to ask him any more questions.

I stood on the platform, resolving to show off the seams

of my blue net stockings and thinking about the power of the House Un-American Activities Committee to make people upset. It seemed something like the war—a force large, far away, and unpredictable, changing shape when you turned your back on it.

The next night I sat in Henry's office reading *Newsweek*. He had sent me inside to warm up. "Your goose bumps are as blue as your bally suit. Go take the frost off."

He stayed out front making his continuous spiel. He thought silence was bad once the show was on. "Here you are, ladies and gentlemen, sexual experimentation and sexual invention, explored, explored . . ."

There wasn't much in *Newsweek* except a picture-spread on Congress, with a shot of Jerry Shaughnessey reading a book. I was staring at this when I began to hear sirens. They got louder and closer, and ground to a halt in our street.

I put on my coat and went out. Henry was staring at a black police car. "Shit," he said.

Four policemen climbed out of the car. One of them beckoned to Henry; I sat down on the bally steps. The policemen's official outfits made them look especially bulky. They slouched and chewed and talked to Henry; they stuck their thumbs under their gun belts.

After a while Henry came toward me and said, "Okay, Babe, they'll hang around for a while; we'll do a show like usual." Under his breath he added, "Tame, honey, *tame*, comprenney?"

Henry edited his spiel. Every time the word *sexual* would have occurred he said *intellectual* instead. The police watched us for only one show and looked bored; they talked to Henry and then started upstairs. Henry gloomily

watched the backs of their polished belts. "Hell. All because some little bint was careless."

He explained that one of the Dreamtown girls had been
stupid. What had she done? Nothing. Never mind what
she'd done. She was stupid. "None of our business. But
every time they come around, it costs."

He tapped his billfold pocket and looked sad.

I wasn't surprised the next week when Henry said we
would have to close the show. The nights had gotten
colder and business was bad. He left me up on my ladder
for only five minutes at a time; he was making his spiel to
an almost empty street.

"This is the way it always goes," he said. "Every year.
The suckers get too cold to stand around and gawk at stuff
in bottles."

He chewed on his unlit cigar. "And of course the cops
didn't help all that much with their visit. So, Starbright,
I'm sorry."

"That's okay."

"What will you do?"

"I don't know. I'll find something."

"Going back to French Bore?"

"No, I won't go back to French Ford."

Henry chewed some more on his cigar. "You been okay,
Sugarbelle, not exactly great, but okay. And it wasn't because of you-know."

You-know was sex. "I would never fire a babe for hanging on to her cherry." He surveyed me sadly. "Cherry is
very important. You are right to value it."

"I guess I shouldn't work for Dreamtown."

"No, sweetheart, you should *not*."

He sat back, looking cross-eyed at his dead cigar. The street was quiet and cold. A hawk flew over, low, and hung above the Fun Show. There were a lot of hawks on the outskirts of Reno. "One nice thing about this show here is that there aren't any animals when you got to close her up. One year, with a different show, I had a python. Hell of a job getting rid of that damn snake."

Henry said he would pay me for the day; he said I should take the rest of the day off. "Because I think you are sincere and are a lady. That's very unusual for me. Usually, with me, it's no work, no pay."

I walked slowly back to Mrs. Rose's, kicking gravel and match folders. Apparently it was possible to feel sad about losing your job at Henry's Permanent Fun Show. My list of things to feel sad about in life was going to be long, I thought.

The next morning I got up early and went out for breakfast. The nearby diner was named Angel's; it had a jukebox that played hillbilly music and Basque music. Basque music had a Spanish rhythm, but the words were in an eccentric language that contained many *r*'s and *z*'s. Angel, a plump cheerful redhead, explained that the Basques had settled in Nevada to be sheepherders; most of these Basques lived in the middle of the state, but there was a small colony in Reno.

At Angel's I ordered pineapple-pecan pancakes, put a nickel in the jukebox for "Down on the Levee," and settled down with the want-ad section of the *Reno Observer*.

What I liked about "Down on the Levee" was the refrain, "Hang your head over/Hear that train go." I had been awakening during the night at Mrs. Rose's thinking I

had heard the one a.m. downhill train; then I had to remind myself that I wasn't in French Ford and I hadn't
heard it. Maybe there was an auditory memory similar to
the visual one and perhaps you carried those scraps of
sound around with you, waiting to be activated.

The want ads had some possibilities:

*GIRLS to distribute route premiums. No experience
necessary $ $ $*

*WANTED   Sincere intelligent young woman to help a
literary gentleman in his work*

*HOSTESSES HOSTESSES HOSTESSES Beautiful,
unconventional, good dancers. Nice hours. Bonuses.*

*WAITRESSES   Experienced, fast. Excellent tips. High-
powered casino.*

GIRLS to make peanut butter sandwiches

The peanut butter sandwich ad appealed to me because
it seemed like a job anybody could do, and also because I
couldn't figure out exactly what it was. (A woman wearing
an apron stood in a spotless country kitchen; in front of
her was a great stack of sliced bread. Did everybody in
Reno eat peanut butter sandwiches?)

I was suspicious of the literary gentleman, whose ad
sounded like the beginning of a horror thriller. The hostesses were Dreamtown, and the waitresses were highly
skilled, which I was not. The route premiums, now . . .
Those multiple dollar signs bothered me. Henry would
have referred to the route premiums as an act or a gig or a
con or a scheme or a game. The route premium game. I
was sure I had heard him talk about it.

141

I looked in my purse. I had twenty-eight dollars; I had paid the rent through the end of the week.

"Hang your head over/Hear the wind blow," the jukebox said. People in songs often felt lost and rootless; it must be an ordinary human condition. I would spend the morning looking at daytime Reno, which I had not seen.

Two divorcées stood on the bridge over the Truckee River pretending to pitch their wedding rings into the water.

I had read an article that said that they were really throwing dimestore rings bought in the Woolworth's on Second Street.

Their wide skirts blew around them and the sleeves of their blouses belled out. Four little boys lounged, watching. One of them finally asked, "Lady, is that your truly ring?"

One divorcée was short and gray-haired; one was tall and athletic. The tall one said, "Yeh, kid. You bet. Worth hundreds, believe me, hundreds. But easy come, easy go, that's what I say." She turned to me. "The only thing I got out of it was two kids."

"Two kids," I said, to keep the conversation going.

"They were all right." She picked a rock up off the bridge and chucked it after her Woolworth ring. "Guess what I got for my real ring? Twenty-five bucks. I ask you. You like a cup of coffee?"

While we had coffee we talked about her children. They were with her mother in Sandusky, Ohio. She was going back there after her divorce.

Sandusky, Ohio, was mostly factories, she said, and the

houses were joined together on the sides. "I like that about here. All the houses in their own little yards."

After I left her I wandered slowly, spending time in front of the pawnshops. These were nice old-fashioned ones with red-painted fronts and gold-lettered signs; I stood at their windows listing the objects and trying to figure out who had owned them and how, in some gambling game, the person had rushed out to pawn that particular possession. The rings, the cameras, the binoculars, those were easy to think about. But who, and when, had owned and lost the silver comb studded with turquoise or the Chinese embroidered coat; who had mortgaged the five-foot dollhouse, a replica of a Colonial mansion, its front half ajar to reveal an upstairs bathroom with a claw-footed tub? I liked the doll's mansion so much that I went in to ask the price; it was five hundred dollars.

That night I dreamed that Steve and I lived in the dollhouse mansion. It was the right size for us, but like the real mansion in the pawnshop window, the dream one had no inside staircase. Steve was upstairs and I was downstairs; all night I tried to fly or climb up the open front of the house to get to him.

Like all my dreams about Steve, this one woke me up so that I couldn't get back to sleep.

I felt cross about this. I was going to the peanut butter sandwich factory in the morning, and I wanted to look ready for whatever it was they did.

Dear Evva:
Do you remember that song about, "The worms crawl in, the worms crawl out"? We were singing it at work

today. One of the things that makes my peanut butter job bearable is that singing is encouraged; Miss Peabody read somewhere that Productivity is Higher When Workers Sing. She likes songs like "Let Me Call You Sweetheart" and "Blue Moon"; they broadcast these at us over the loudspeaker.

"The Worms" happened after a squirter yelled out that she had found a worm in her peanut butter. She was lying. A worm would be too mashed by the time it got to the peanut butter to be identifiable.

A squirter is someone who squirts peanut butter at a cracker that travels by on a rubber assembly belt. I am a squirter. The person on one side of me lines the crackers up on the belt and the person on the other side slaps another cracker on top of the one I have squirted, and someone further down the line puts these crackers into a packaging machine. Packaging is skilled, and gets paid two cents an hour more than squirting. The job is not as boring as it sounds, because if you figure out a rhythm, and sing, you forget where you are, and you squirt and sing and squirt and sing. It is a jolt when the hose gets clogged or the peanut butter runs out and you have to stop working for a while.

We get all the free peanut butter crackers we want during the day, but they stop us if we try to take them home; they're afraid we'll sell them.

I think a lot about you and home and everyone, and sometimes I get a specific physical memory . . .

I stopped writing and looked at this and recognized that Evva, who was still living in French Ford, didn't want to hear about how much I missed it. I put a period after *memory* and went on. *Thank you for the good letter and*

144

the fifty from Daddy. Write more. Last letter was NOT SUFFICIENTLY DETAILED. Love, love, love

There were two worst things about the peanut butter job. One was the hour at which we had to be at work: seven-thirty. Sometimes at home I got up early. But getting up to pull a time-clock lever in a peanut butter sandwich factory was different. None of the other girls cared about this problem; when I talked about it they looked at me and moved their shoulders as if that was the way life was.

The other awful thing was the free evenings. Working for Henry there had not been free evenings. But the peanut butter sandwich plant shut down at four-thirty; then there was a whole empty rest of the day, with an empty dinner hour and a vacant space later, and at the bottom of all that Mrs. Rose's wetmop porch and Mrs. Rose too, fat, light-footed, snooping around my door.

It was too early for the Casino bar, it even seemed early for Woolworth's.

One evening I walked down to the end of Wasatch Street, to the place where it hit the mountain. Most of the houses on Wasatch Street looked like Mrs. Rose's, made of overlapping asphalt shingles and painted in light colors, but there was an occasional innovative adobe and once even a brick house. The street ended at a dry gully with a bench to sit down on and a place to rest your feet while you watched the mountain and the opposite dry bank with its row of manzanita bushes.

It was still light when I got back to my room, and I walked to the crooked dresser with its flat crazy mirror and stared at my face. Even with the mirror distortion I saw it was a face that a lot of people would like, and I thought that I ought not to be working in a peanut butter sandwich factory.

I walked around the room and debated this for a while, and it still seemed to be true. Finally I hung my purse over my shoulder and went outside. I was going down to the Greyhound Bus Station to get a schedule for buses to French Ford.

All the way downtown I thought about arriving home, about getting off the bus at the red dusty place where the Greyhound made its French Ford stop, hoisting my suitcase out and walking down the hill toward town. In this fantasy it was summer again and I walked down the hill getting the fronts of my sandals and the tips of my toes powdered with red dust. I didn't ask myself whether I would meet Steve or not. It was summer, and during last summer things had been okay, or almost okay; and maybe, for the space of this imagination, I trusted Steve again.

The Reno bus station looked peculiar; I had not been in it since the night I arrived. I tried to identify the places where I had stood and thought and sat that evening. Then I got a schedule and went into the lunch counter.

"Read up." "Read down." Bus schedules were difficult for people with low mechanical aptitude. Miss Peabody had explained that low mechanical aptitude involved poor spatial orientation. It meant you couldn't hit the cracker with the squirter.

The other customers at the counter were silent; they leaned their elbows on the counter and stared into their coffee cups. I ordered coffee and settled down to think

146

some more about arriving in French Ford. I placed myself at the bottom of the hill with my suitcase set down in the dust and my arms open to greet Sybil and Mrs. Farmer or whoever might be coming out of the General Store.

"Hi," I was saying excitedly, "hi, oh hi!" and, "Grace, darling!" the people were saying. I thought about this and liked it a lot and drank my coffee. It was hot in my fantasy of French Ford, and the smell was the usual one of pine, laurel, asphalt, and dust.

The voice that interrupted me was not the kind of voice you expect to hear at a lunch counter. It was a preaching voice, pitched at a declamatory level, with heavy rhythmic intonations. It belonged to a man who stood four seats down, leaning over the person on the stool.

"Death," he said, "and all around me, Death. And a person jumps out the hotel window. And my tears fall on the pages of the book."

The man next to me didn't budge, nor did the one after that; both of them kept their noses buried in their coffee cups and stared at the marble countertop. The preacher leaned over the shoulder of the man farther down the line and said, "And the book was the mighty book that had the truth therein." He took his coat off and dropped it on the floor.

Under his coat he was wearing a purple cocktail dress with a boned top. His corrugated hairy chest and broad shoulders stuck out above the top of the dress, which had no shoulder straps. "The great whore of Babylon beckoned me with her manicured finger," he said.

The person he was talking to didn't look up. "Yeah, Sidney, yeah."

The man next to me shifted his position to include me. He was a Greyhound bus driver and wore the usual uniform. "He is nuts," he said.

"Yes."

"But that *did* happen to him. Someone jumped."

I murmured something.

"A cartwheel of fire with the face of an angel," the preacher said.

"Poetic, kind of," the bus driver told me.

"Yes."

The preacher began his story again. "Death. And all around me, Death . . ."

"The funny thing is how it hits people," the bus driver said. "Tragedy, like he had. The thing is, you shouldn't give in."

"Yes."

"But he had this real tragedy. He was holding onto this guy's foot over Heidelberg. And he lost his grip. The guy went right through the bomb bay."

"That was terrible."

"Yeah, terrible."

The transvestite wore purple eyeshadow and magenta lipstick; some of his nails had been enamelled silver, the rest were unvarnished and black-rimmed. He wore a ring with a red stone. I asked, "Why does he dress like a woman?"

The bus driver sighed. "No real reason. That's just how it hit him."

I stared at the preacher and wondered if I would find him less sad if he looked attractive in his purple dress. He was sitting on a stool now, leaning forward, drinking hot water. His empty boned dress jutted over the counter.

The bus driver got up and straightened his jacket. He was an older bus driver with bushy gray hair and a fat face. "The thing is, it's different for different people. Giving in."

I agreed, and he said, "Have a good trip to wherever you're going."

The transvestite said, "This hot water is swell," in a reasonable voice, and I told the bus driver thank you.

On the way back to Mrs. Rose's I remembered an article I had read about a psychologist whose motto was "One day at a time." I decided this was a good motto for me. It was thinking about a whole series of days that made them difficult.

It was pretty clear to me that I couldn't go back to French Ford. I wasn't sure whether I really regarded that as giving in or not, but I didn't want to do it any more, at least not tonight.

16

By the next week there was a cliff of snow in front of Mrs. Rose's house and the wetmop porch was covered with ice. When I was dressed and had pulled the shade up it was still dark; the porch light made streaks on the ice. Someone had shovelled a canyon through the snow, and a man was sitting on the steps with his back to me and his feet in the canyon.

I put on my Salvation Army coat and snowboots and clumped out on the porch, trying to figure out who the navy-blue canvas back belonged to. At first I had thought of Steve, and then decided the shoulders were not right for Steve, and after that I thought of Henry, but Henry was fatter. And then the man turned around and he was David McCracken. "Hi," he said. My foot slipped on the ice; he reached out and caught me.

We stayed that way for a minute, he supporting me by one elbow; I staring down, he looking up. He said, "I thought you wouldn't ever come out." We righted ourselves and he came up on the porch and held his face down; his cheeks gave off a frosty warm fog.

David's face looked pulled and his eyes had shadows under them; even so, the first thing I thought was *how young he is,* the cheeks with that rose-flush, the eye-whites so white; I had been looking mostly at Henry recently.

He said, "Evva gave me your address. Let's have breakfast." I slipped again and he put his arm around me, and we went down the stairs that way, linked, with a frosty cloud of breath traveling in front of us.

"There's a diner," I told him. "Angel's. That's the owner's name: Angel."

The snow on the sidewalk had a crust on it; we matched steps. David said Angel did not seem a name for a diner owner, and we tried to come up with diner-owner names: Sam's and Sue's, Dad's and Nell's. David squeezed my hand. "Maybe this will all be okay."

I didn't ask him what would be okay. I thought he meant something about me.

Angel's had only eight booths, each one with a jukebox and a fruit machine. We sat down, and Angel, who was wearing a pink uniform today, took our orders. David said, "You haven't asked why I'm here."

"To see me?"

He shook his head and stared at me intently, as if I should be understanding something. I stared back. He said, "It's about Lenny Barr Dowell."

"Lenny Barr? In the French Ford grocery store?"

"Yes."

"What about him?"

David said, oh, you haven't talked to anybody, and I

said, not for a couple of days, and he said, well, there's no way you could know then, and I said, Know what?

"He's dead." David's voice caught between "he's" and "dead." I didn't say, "Dead, what do you mean, dead?" or "How awful, how?" I was thinking these things; it has to be upsetting to learn that someone you have known all your life has suddenly stopped being. But there was more here than that; something extra. David waited.

"He was shot," he said finally.

"Shot?" It sounded peculiar, a short, strange word in a foreign language.

"Yeah. Shot."

"My God. How?"

"Someone tried to get gas out of the grocery store pump. And the siren went off. And Lenny came. And there was some kind of . . ."

"Fight," I supplied.

"Yeah. Fight."

"And what happened?"

"He was shot. He's dead." He slumped his forehead onto his hand.

I stared at him, and then I began to get it. "David," I said. "Your brothers?"

He shook his head, looking down.

"Somehow . . ." I said.

"Nobody knows who did it."

I reached for his hand; and after a while he let me hold it. Then he started to talk. "Jesus, Grace, Jesus. When it started up . . ."

"Yes."

"I was up there for the day. To help Buddy with his unemployment stuff. And then I hung around with them, and they got really *drunk*. Not mean, just dumb. You know the way they get."

"Yes."

"Yelling around and acting dumb. Pretending the gas pump was the enemy. Yelling, 'Come out of there, you fucking cheating lousy Jap gas pump.'

"And then Argo shot the Texaco sign full of holes. And the burglar alarm went off. Lenny Barr came up out of Deep Creek Road in his Jeep. And my brothers . . .'"

I got up and moved around the table to the seat beside him. At first he wouldn't push over to let me in, and then he did.

"My brothers," he said again. David was a lot bigger than I, and it was hard to embrace him. I put one arm across his chest and one behind his shoulders. Finally he relaxed and leaned against me. We were that way when Angel brought our pancakes.

"Hey," she told us, "you kids ought to rent a park bench." But she left our two plates of pancakes together on the same side of the table and came back and gave us more coffee and made clucking noises.

I waited a while after she had gone and then said, "Lenny got out of the Jeep?"

"Yes. Jesus. It was awful. You know that dream where you can't move."

"Yes."

"I thought there must be something I could do, and I couldn't think what it was and I waited for something to happen . . .

"And then it happened, and everybody just stood there. And it was as if it hadn't really happened at all. Except that Lenny . . .'"

"Was he lying on the ground?"

"He was holding onto the gas pump. With his arms around it. And then he just slowly slid down . . ."

David pulled loose from me while he told me this. "Oh, my God," he said.

"It doesn't seem real. I forget about it, and all of a sudden I remember."

"I'm sorry," I said. "I'm so sorry." After a while I said, "There's got to be something you can do."

"Those dumb jerks. Those dopes."

"Maybe you can say you saw and it was an accident. Somebody's hand slipped."

"Those *dopes*."

"You were across the street; you were watching; one of them had this gun."

"I wasn't across the street."

"They were going deer hunting."

"You don't hunt deer with a pistol."

I touched David's cheek; it was wet. He moved and I felt his cheek, wet, through the shoulder of my sweater.

"You can't believe, Grace. I love them."

"Of course I believe it."

"They're my brothers."

"I know."

"They were *for* me. When I was little. They really tried . . . One night Dad was really drunk . . ."

I smoothed his shoulder, first the knob at the top, then down over the arm.

"Dad grabbed this chair and held it over his head, he said, 'I'll break every bone in your body, you rotten snivelling little bastard . . .'

"And then Lloyd came in and grabbed him; Lloyd was

only fourteen; he wasn't anywhere near as big as Dad was . . ."

I touched his shoulder some more. "I'm sorry."

He put his arm around me. The jukebox, which had been silent until now, whirred and began the first bars of "Careless Love." Angel squeaked up on rubber-soled shoes.

When she was gone David said, "I think, maybe, if I hide out they won't have much evidence.

"Of course everybody in town will know," he went on. "The whole damn town will know. Who else would do that? But they won't really have evidence."

"They won't know anything. French Ford won't want it to be someone from town. They'll want them to be from somewhere else."

After a minute David said, "Grace, maybe we'd better go back to your room. I feel tired."

We picked our way across Mrs. Rose's porch, between the wetmop, the bucket, and the shovel. My room was a small tan one, the wallpaper speckled and tortured to look like oatmeal and the floor laid out in linoleum squares that simulated wood. The only furniture was a single bed with a white chenille spread, a cardboard dresser and mirror, a hotplate, and a wicker armchair. I liked the wicker armchair because it looked like the one that had sat on our back porch at home.

I took David's coat. "You should lie down." He murmured about the landlady, and I lied, "I never see her."

He lay down on the bed and I went to the corner to call Mom's Yummies, which was the name of the peanut butter sandwich people. When I came back David was asleep, flat on his back, his profile pointing at the ceiling, his hands crossed on his chest. He looked like a crusader on a tomb. All he needed was a dog to lie crosswise at his feet.

I sat in the wicker armchair and chewed on the corners of my fingernails and tried to think what might happen next.

There were several possibilities, all bad.

Item one was my lie about Mrs. Rose, the light-footed snooping landlady. People might think that a Reno landlady wouldn't mind a man in your bed, but those people would be wrong. Reno was half gambling houses and divorces and half Calvinists who were extra strict to make up for the other stuff. Mrs. Rose belonged to this latter group.

Item two was a set of unanswerable questions about French Ford, like, how much did the police suspect? Did they suspect only David's brothers, or were they wondering about David too?

And item three was Mom's Yummies; Miss Peabody had sounded cross about my day off. She knew I wasn't a devoted squirter.

I left David and went downtown to the library, where I read Proust and chewed some more on my fingernail corners.

When I got back to the room David was propped up against a mound of pillows and couch cushions, reading yesterday's paper. He smiled at me; he looked better; he had lost the circles from under his eyes.

"No," he said, "uh-uh; you're not getting it; it's not that I'm a fugitive; I just don't want to be questioned."

I sat down in the wicker armchair and fooled with the ends of my bitten fingers. "There's got to be something."

156

"No there doesn't."

"There's *always* something."

"No there's not."

He looked relaxed about this. How could he be relaxed? Yes, he said, he would call the Congressman's office, not to ask for help, just to say he wouldn't be in. They wouldn't care; he was un unpaid college intern.

"What about your college?" I asked. "What about the Friends' School, what about . . . what about . . . ?"

David moved his shoulders. "*I'm* worried about my brothers."

"And you? What about you?"

"I'll be all right."

"But David. You're only nineteen." Nineteen had seemed young when applied to myself: Here you are, I'd been telling myself, only nineteen, bumping around Reno, working at these idiotic jobs. Nineteen seemed worse when it was attached to someone else.

David grinned. "God. Isn't it awful."

When we had laughed some he said, "Seriously, though, I've got to move on. I can't stay."

"I like having you here."

"I'll bet."

"You could stay lots longer."

"Let's go out to dinner."

I wondered about money, because neither of us seemed to have any, but he said, "I noticed a place that advertises 'Languorous Cocktail Snax.' I think what that means is free meatballs. You buy just one drink and you get to go up to a smorgasbord table."

Walking along Reno Street with David felt good. Suddenly it didn't feel like *Alone in Reno* or *After Steve* but like *Life,* not the magazine kind. The street was brightly lit and interesting and we were going to a place where you could get a free dinner: sausages, meatballs, sliced ham, sliced turkey, a whole entire meal for just one drink.

We went into the bar holding hands and the waitress gave us her best table by the window with a view of the people jostling by on the pavement. We sat there and laughed and talked about the French Ford School when we were nine years old.

"You had that hair down your back, like the curtain pull," David said, and I knew what he meant. The curtain pull in our classroom had been made of fiberglass and had a white, unreal gloss along it.

"Well, you had those great blue jeans. I was jealous of those blue jeans that were so stiff they would stand by themselves." I wondered, as I said this, if it were insulting. But David agreed, "Yes, they were great."

We must have looked like an ad for good times: "Good Living in the Postwar Era," sitting in the window, flushed and hand-holding, tilted forward on our white enamel modern-museum chairs. The waitress brought us a free drink, "From Robbie; he's the boss." We drank Robbie's health.

"We look good together," I said, and David asked, "Is *that* what you've been sitting here thinking?" and I said, "Yes, yes, it is."

On the way home we suddenly began talking seriously. Maybe it was the effect of the cold air, the piled snow, the too-sharp street shadows. "They'll be embarrassed," David told me. He meant that the Congressman's office would be embarrassed by his crazy brothers who had shot someone. "The social worker will be embarrassed. The

Congressman, too. Sue won't be embarrassed. She'll be sorry."

"And Steve?"

"Steve? Maybe Steve will think it's funny."

Yes, Steve might think that. Or, he might be very, very sympathetic. At the bottom of my life, like a shark in a swimming pool, he lurked, Steve, the white swimmer. The swimming pool that I was putting the shark in was the Deep Sink, where David and I had sat and talked and recited the poem about the man of double deed.

When we got back to my room I suggested that David sleep in the bed and I on the floor, but he said, "*Grace*. What's wrong with you?" so emphatically that I gave in right away.

"Jeez, I'm tired." David stretched; I watched the armpit: evenly furred dark hair against tan body; shiny and clean, like the rest of him.

The next morning Mrs. Rose unlocked the door with her key and stood in the doorway with her legs apart. "I'm asking you to leave, Miss Dowell."

It took me a while to understand. I propped myself on one elbow. "This is a friend who is spending the night."

It was too dark to see Mrs. Rose clearly. "By twelve o'clock."

"Mrs. Rose," I said, "don't I have the right to have a guest?"

"I will give you a refund for three days' rent." She paused in the doorway. "If you are here after twelve o'clock I will call the police."

No one said anything, and she went on out and slammed the door, not relocking it.

David and I got dressed and went to Angel's, where we talked until Angel heard us and came over. "That mean-minded bitch," she said. "I knew her in school; she was a mean-minded bitch then, and she still is. You kids stick together. Two's better than one."

We looked at each other. We were eating pancakes again. "It would be dangerous for you, Grace."

"Not for me. You're the one."

I got out my Greyhound bus schedule. The next big stop after Reno was Winnemucca, Nevada. There were some little places in between, but they sounded too anonymous to be places where you could live.

"Winnemucca," I said. "It means something good in some Indian language."

David said, "And it costs only four dollars to get there."

He looked excited; I felt that way, too. It was one thing to run away from home; it was entirely different if you had a friend with you.

17

The Greyhound bus let us out in Winnemucca in front of the Bob Cat Casino.

The major feature of the Bob Cat Casino, and of Winnemucca, was the bobcat; he was a block long and was spread across the front of the casino building and was made of rows and rows of electric light bulbs. He stood crouched, ready to leap; the plateglass windows and doors were arranged between his front and back legs. During the daytime we were to discover that the bobcat was red, but at night only his nostrils and eartips were red and the rest of him was the usual bright-yellow electric color.

Somewhere in the Bob Cat's promotional literature was a statement that their cat contained more light bulbs than any other artifact in the world.

David and I stood side by side, staring up at the dazzle. Behind us the Greyhound idled loudly. The sidewalk was crowded although it was eleven at night; there was some snow.

"We could get back on the bus," I said. Neither of us

could remember the name of the next town on the bus route. Also, we were low on money. David picked up our suitcase and said, "Let's walk."

As soon as we had left Route 40 and its electric lights we could see the sky, jammed and crammed with stars, and ahead of us the single row of mountains that paralleled the town. A brilliant moon polished the white mountaintops and white fields. To the right was the Roundup Motel, red and blue signs alternating, the red sign saying Open and the blue one saying Rooms. The reflection of the letters made shiny colored smears on the snow.

I tried to figure out how many times I had moved in the last month; if you counted the trip to San Francisco as the first time it was four moves now. That wasn't very dramatic; a lot of people traveled all the time because of their jobs. But not me. I had lived in the same room in the same house forever. I knew every inch of that house backward. I started remembering it: white front hall with brown mahogany table, green living room with white books, green dining room with porcelain chandelier, yellow kitchen . . . When I got to the back porch and its mockingbird I let go of my part of the suitcase handle.

"What's the matter?" David asked.

I had started thinking of Daddy; I had put him on the back porch. I said, "Oh, my God. Poor Daddy."

David set the suitcase down.

He said, "Hey, Grace."

"Yes."

"We can't afford two rooms."

"No."

"We could ask for two *beds*."

"The hell with it."

162

I looked out across the back side of Winnemucca, a wide flat sparkling plain that spread into Wyoming on our left and ended on our right where the Roundup Motel flicked its raw neon words. Ahead of us the mountains were a wall against the invader. The town was three streets wide and ended in wilderness. "One bed will be fine. For Christ's sake. I'm freezing."

I didn't usually swear, and the word *Christ* hung in the air, frozen. Sections of breath, too, had frozen. In a moment they would fall to the ground as irregularly shaped ice fragments. "Let's go."

David said, "Okay, then," and we picked up the suitcase and crunched some more across the snow toward the motel, a fade-out from the end of a wartime movie about refugees forcing their way into the future.

During the bus ride to Winnemucca David and I had sat facing each other like two question marks, I sideways in the seat with my knees up and my nose near his shoulder. I had talked, partly about Reno, partly about French Ford.

David was the one who mentioned Steve. "Are you afraid of him?"

"Yes."

"Would he come after you?"

"Yes."

"Do you love him?"

"I used to."

David didn't pursue this.

What will make me stop loving Steve? I wondered.

I moved the conversation on to David's life. I asked him about running away when he was nine and staying in the diggings. I liked to think about David in the diggings,

163

small and lonely and scared. And then his mother coming
with a flashlight. "Boy, that night she told me I was going
to the Settlement, I thought, this is going to end. I'm going
someplace. I'll live like a person."

"And you kissed her and hugged her."

"I was mad at her; it was only later that I understood."

Outside the bus window, Nevada went by, flat near the
road, mountainous in the distance. The bus traveled fast;
there was no speed limit in Nevada.

The Roundup Motel's room 47 had a cowboy motif—
the lamp stand was the cowboy's horse; the sheets had
alternating boots and saddles stamped along their borders.
I wedged myself against the head of the bed with two
pillows behind me and fooled with the lace on the front of
my bathrobe. David still wore his shirt and pants.

"Listen," he said. "I feel as if you don't want to."

"Why?" I was partly defensive, partly curious.

"You're bent over like your Auntie Sybil."

I pushed my shoulders back.

"All you have to do is say 'no.' "

I felt cross. "I'm ready; I'm sitting here."

David turned and made shoe-untying motions.

I pulled again at the lace. Evva had bought me this robe;
she was critical of my taste in clothes; she thought my
selections were too meek and unassertive.

David undid his belt and began to squeeze out of his
pants. It was hard, I thought, for anyone to undress gracefully. Worse, maybe, for a woman than for a man. Women
had all those makeshift elastic straps and metal studs.
They taught you on the variety stage how to unsnap your

garter suspenders gracefully. I had undressed in the bathroom and hadn't tried to practice any of that on David.

I watched him with my peripheral vision. The tie was
off; he was undoing shirt buttons.

I tried to remember Steve undressing in the graveyard.
He had taken his shirt off fast. I couldn't recall any shirt-
tails.

Here was another piece of bathrobe lace. I pulled
hard.

On the far side of the bed, David gave up on buttons and
reversed the shirt over his head. He wasn't wearing an
undershirt. His back, firm and brown, corded on either
side of a knobbed backbone, appeared first as a quadrilat-
eral slice, then as a whole vulnerable back. After that there
were the arms aloft, with a muscle at the base of each
shoulder. The nicest part of the back was the row of ridges
along the rib cage.

Tug, my second piece of bathrobe lace came loose.
David screwed his shirt into a ball and flung it toward the
bathroom door.

His arms were still in the air when I slid all the way
down in the bed and put the blanket under my chin.
"David?"

"Yes?"

"I can't."

He said, "Oh." He didn't waste time saying, For God's
sake, *now* you tell me. He turned around and held onto the
mattress edge.

"I'm sorry."

He shrugged. It was a nice gesture; he had good coordi-
nation. "It's okay."

165

"I like you, really. I wanted to, really."

"It's *okay*."

He didn't sound irritated; he sounded fine. I opened my mouth to say something more. And then decided: No, Grace, no. Close your mouth.

"Don't worry." David had quit holding the mattress; he reached out and grasped my hand.

I held hands with him until a blur appeared in the part of my vision where the hands should have been. Then I lay down with my face against the pillow. "Damn it," I said. "Damn it, I don't *know* why."

"It doesn't matter."

"It's not *him*. I hate him."

"Grace. It's *okay*."

"I want to, but I just . . ."

"You're scared."

"Yes, scared. David, what's the matter with me?"

Two ponds of tears, round and delineated, shaped themselves on the boot-embroidered pillow case, and spread onto the comforter.

David let go of my hand and touched my shoulder.

I could tell from the way his arm tensed that this contact affected him. I said, "I'm sorry; I'm sorry," and he said, "It's okay; oh, shit," and then he went to sit in the easy chair.

We stayed that way for a while, me lying on my face, feeling as if I had been novocained from head to foot, and David in the chair, silent. Finally he let out a sigh and asked in a peculiar voice, "Did you ever play Famous People?"

I sat up and he was smiling a little. "Come on," he said, "I got to be really good at it when I was in Washington;

the secretaries played all during lunch. They did it with Washington names, but we can play it the regular way."

Famous People is the one where you say, "I am a B," thinking to yourself, Beethoven, Brahms, Botticelli, Bluebeard, or whatever, and the other person has to ask specific questions and gets to ask leading questions if they handle it right.

"Did you have red hair?" David finally wanted to know, and I had to admit that I was Mata Hari. When he was William Penn I said that I didn't think of William Penn as a real person; he was a myth, and David said, "Well, if you had gone to a Quaker school you'd think William Penn was real; we had William Penn every single month."

It was four in the morning when we stopped Famous People. We put the mattress on the floor and I made David take the comforter with the tear stains.

After the lights were out I wanted to get up and go over to him and say I was sorry. But I summoned up Evva's voice to remind me that I thought I could get away with anything; I thought I owned the whole damn world. And after I had told myself this for quite a while, I fell asleep.

18

One of us had to get a job; both of us agreed to this.

David said he should get the job because he had worked for three years now and was more experienced; he had been a waiter, a grocery store clerk, and an intern in Jerry Shaughnessey's office.

I said I should get the job because it was dangerous for him to work at all.

He said he could use a false name. I mentioned social security numbers. He said that the social security filing system was fallible. I said that I would worry about him. Finally he said, "Well, wish me luck, ducks," and kissed me on the cheek and pushed his way through the sidewalk crowd and through the Bob Cat's revolving front door.

I watched the door, with a replica of the cat, spin around after him, and then I leaned against the cement front of the building and watched the people.

Most of them were tourists who had stopped to go to the bathroom and to look at the bobcat. There was a big knot of them along the front of the casino, trying to count the electric light bulbs; the casino offered fifty dollars worth of free play to anybody who got the number of light bulbs right.

There was some hitch to this, because almost no one ever won it.

The people seemed ugly and fat in their heavy winter traveling clothes; they bumped into each other, looked up, yelled numbers, and talked about how much their backs hurt.

There were a few local residents who stood out because they went by purposefully and because they had snow-burned outdoor faces. I had learned to recognize the Basques, and they, especially, seemed different, tall and straight and black and brown, like a grade-school idea of an American Indian.

I admired these occasional Basques for a while, and after about ten minutes I went across the street and into Et-cheverria's, which was a Basque restaurant.

David was disbelieving when we regrouped later. "You mean you just went into a Basque restaurant? And asked for a job? And told him you'd never waitressed before?"

"He asked me some questions."

"Jesus, that's wonderful."

Etcheverria's was dark and had pink tablecloths and a strong smell of fish, olive oil, and garlic. There was only one person in the restaurant; he sat at the table nearest the cash register. It was the only table with a vase of paper flowers on it, so I was pretty sure he was the owner. I walked up beside him and said, "Mr. Etcheverria?"

He had the Basque appearance that I liked, dark and somber. He was about sixty years old, and was a little heavier than most of them.

169

He was eating something red and reading a newspaper. He looked up at me and then went back to his paper.

I had my pocketbook over my shoulder and used that as something to hang on to. "I'd like a job as a waitress."

He took a forkful, chewed it energetically, and spent about thirty seconds examining me. "What makes you think you can waitress? You don't know anything about Basque food: What's *marmitaka*?"

"I don't know."

"How long do you cook *mamiya*?"

"I don't know any of that stuff."

"So why should I hire you?"

I shifted my pocketbook. "I need the job. I'll work hard."

"Um." He surveyed me moodily.

"Sometimes a newcomer does better than the usual people. I move really fast."

He shifted his food from right cheek to left cheek.

"My aunt was a waitress," I added, getting inventive. "It runs in the blood. I know I'll be good at it."

"How would you carry three entrées at the same time?" He seemed pleased with this question and stabbed a fork at his red stew. But when I took a minute to think about it he said, "Listen, I will give this my serious consideration. I may change my mind. But I don't think I'm *for* you." He brooded a bit, chewing hard. "I don't think I will change my mind, either. But come back tomorrow."

I was at the door when he said, "Miss—what's your name?"

I told him Grace, and he said, "Well, Grace, I thought about it and I decided. I *will* give you a chance."

170

"I don't know what got into him," I said to David. "He seems all right, though."

David had a job as a busboy. He was to get forty cents an hour; I would get two dollars a day, plus tips.

"They tip okay in a Basque restaurant," David told me.

I took his hand. Clearly, we had to move out of the Roundup Motel. We had seven dollars between us; neither of us would get paid for a week.

The receptionist at the Roundup said to go to Mrs. Sanchez's on Baud Street. "It's clean, and a lot of places aren't. You kids got jobs?"

Yes, we had jobs. "Good for you," the receptionist said.

Mrs. Sanchez was a round sandy lady with mascara'd eyelashes and a Southern accent.

"No, dear," she said, answering my unasked question, "Mr. Sanchez wasn't a Mexican gentleman; he was a Basque gentleman; he was very handsome; some Basque gentlemen are, you know."

She spoke so admiringly of Mr. Sanchez that I thought she must be a widow and still in love with him, but she said, "My goodness, no, dear; he was a traveling man, and finally, he simply traveled; good riddance. I suppose you would like to see my Aqua Room, it is by far my best one. First, it is aqua, which is a flattering color, especially to one of your complexion. And secondly, it is farther from the bathroom. Some people think of next to the bathroom as the best place, but they are wrong; they are forgetting about the constant flushing. I am happy that you are to have the room."

She moved the eyelashes, which were white at the bottoms, although dark at the tips. "You children are so sweet together. It makes me feel sad, sort of."

"Oh, we're okay, Mrs. Sanchez." I wasn't sure what I was answering when I said this.

There were three other people rooming at Mrs. Sanchez's; on the first floor was Mr. Dodd ("rhymes with God, dear; easy to remember"), who was bent and wiry and whose room was piled with salvaged pieces of metal: wire loops, wheels, handles, bicycle chains.

"I like tenants who are neat," Mrs. Sanchez said, "but after a while you get fond of anyone. And he's lived here for five years; he pays his rent on time; he's on social security."

The second floor held, down the hall from us, a middle-aged couple who sat in their room in the evening and drank. They weren't noisy drinkers, except that sometimes someone in their room would drop a glass object. And after they had used the bathroom it smelled of red wine. I fantasized that it was their pee that gave the bathroom its red-wine smell, but when I watched for signs of this chemical persistence in my own system I didn't find it.

At night, after the lights were out, David and I talked.

"How was your day?" he would say, and I would say, "Okay, here, have half a meat loaf sandwich."

Both of us got off work at ten. In another week we would begin meeting at the casino restaurant for supper after work. But that first week we were still poor; it seemed safer to come back to our room.

"This meat loaf is good," David said.

"It's Basque meat loaf. It has a lot of onions in it."

"Jeez." There were crinkly sounds as David used his

stack of paper napkins. "The murder was in the Sacramento paper today . . ."

"Yes?" I'd been afraid to ask him about this.

"Nothing. There are some suspects. Whereabouts not known."

"Oh."

"It's moved down into the county news now. Placer County. French Ford killing. Police hunt suspects."

We were silent for a while. "Does it give you a stomach-ache?" I asked.

"Yes. And that word *hunt*. As if they had dogs." There was a metallic noise of mattress springs; David was turning over. He was on his mattress on the floor. The light in the room was dim, but I could see that he had stretched out on his stomach, his face in his arms. "Tell me about your job," he said in a muffled voice.

I tried to describe Mr. Etcheverria, excited and argumentative, and Mrs. Etcheverria, excited and muddled. "She told me to put boiling water in it and it broke. Thank God he was watching. They're nice, really. They asked me to call them Mr. E. and Mrs. E. Do you feel better?"

"Yeah. It comes and goes."

I wanted to put my arms around him. "Tell me about *your* job."

His job was simple, he said; it was clearing tables and collecting trays. He worked with a waitress named Jen.

"Is she pretty?"

"Yes."

"Do you like her?"

"Sure."

I changed the subject. It was dark, and it seemed a good time to ask this. I asked David what he believed in.

173

"Huh?"

"Do you *believe* in something?" I didn't feel like explaining that Steve had said, *I want to believe in something*.

David said that he did. He believed that human beings could improve during their lifetimes. He believed in social legislation and social change. He believed in the greatest good for the greatest number. He believed in love. He said these things out into the dark without sounding self-conscious about them.

"You sound like Jerry Shaughnessey." I was remembering Reveille and Steve's speech to the locomotive. David said, "That's okay. Jerry's an honest politician."

I was surprised. I had accepted Steve's evaluation of Jerry Shaughnessey.

After a while I asked David if he knew why he believed all this so cleanly and firmly and he said that he did.

"I was poor, and I thought and wondered. And then, there was all that Socialist stuff around French Ford. Even if the Socialists were rich."

I was silent, remembering that the Dowells were the Socialists who were rich. "Believe it or not," David said, "well, sure you'll believe it; why not—Steve shaped my thoughts some. You know, Steve is always reading political theory. Fooling around with it. I don't know what it means for him."

"Neither does he."

"Something to fool around with . . . And then the Friends; they're concerned about a lot of issues. And finally, there was my mother."

I was surprised into a question. "Your mother?"

"Yes. My mother was always reading. Late at night, she was always reading."

I had never thought of Sue Ann McCracken as reading. Perhaps it was the eyes with the big circles under them, and the fragile body frame; she looked deprived, that was it. I lay, hearing Evva's voice, "You Dowells . . ."

"About Steve," I said, "I think he kind of believed in it. The political theory."

"Well, I thought that, too. He'd go along believing for a while. And then he'd get ironic."

"What kind of ironic?"

"Nothing lasts. There aren't any absolutes. Trust is abdication. The greatest good is . . ."

"Betraying your best friend. Oh my God, David."

"Yeah, that was bad."

"It makes me want to throw up."

There was a problem about exchanging confidences like this with David. A warm trusting feeling shaped itself in the room, an atmosphere of possibility that made me want to climb down onto David's mattress with him. And we'd signed a compact not to do that, hadn't we? I, especially, had signed that compact. Maybe Steve had marked me permanently.

David crunched around on his mattress for quite a while that night before he fell asleep.

Dear Evva:
Well, I am sorry about not writing all that time, and sorry about you worrying . . .

Evva was the only person whom I could talk to about being with David. It was hard, in a letter, to go into all the ins and outs of this. Evva, are you still in love with Lloyd McCracken? Do you know where he is now?

David and I get along very well . . .

I wasn't going to tell Evva that David and I had started out to sleep together, and that I hadn't been able to do it.

We each have jobs, and it is a funny feeling, living together in an aqua bedroom in Winnemucca; not anything like your and my dream of marriage that we talked about in Placer High, more like something from a children's story. I reread this and crossed out the last phrase. Evva wouldn't understand about the children's story; "Hansel and Gretel" maybe it was supposed to be.

Evva, I want to talk to you.

I couldn't call Evva on the telephone any more, because a telephone call might be dangerous for David.

We have an aqua bedroom with white curtains with aqua spots on them. We are pretending, first to be married and then to be grown-up; I keep being afraid someone is going to find us out and separate us.

Oh, my God; poor Evva; what a load of stuff.

I wanted to tell Evva about our late night dinners in the casino café, but that description seemed too complicated.

I know you don't believe me, but I miss all of you all the time; I dream about you, I mean about YOU; let me know if there is any news about the boys; I mean, THE BOYS. And I think of you, I think of you. And love, love, love.

I rolled my finger across the end of my pen and made a fingerprint to press on the bottom of the letter. When Evva and I wrote to each other in grade school she used to put a print at the bottom of the letter; she would grab a cat, one of hers or one of Mrs. Farmer's, and put its paw in the ink, and use that for a signature stamp.

I folded the letter and wiped my finger with cold cream and had the impulse to reach out and say, "Hold me, David," but decided absolutely against that. David smiled at me and gave me a thumbs-up sign, and that had to be enough.

I had begun having a new kind of dream, one that I associated with David, even though he didn't appear in it. This was a dream about motion—dancing, skiing, driving a car; one night it was gliding; Daddy had given me a glider ride once for my birthday; I remembered how the plane paused before it cleared its tow, then settled onto an air current, the yellow country below us and the blue air shining through the fragile wings.

I thought about David when I woke up from this dream and wanted to share with him the wonderful feeling of triumph. And then I didn't say anything about it at all.

David and I were now going every night to the casino coffee shop, where Jen, the waitress who worked with David, babied us with stolen food. She brought us the leftover shrimp from the expensive restaurant on the other side of the casino. "Here you are, young lovers, giant shrimp, eat them fast before the boss comes." Jen wore a purple evening gown slit up one side to her waist; when she leaned over the table her breasts tried to fall out of the divided front of her dress.

The jukebox played "Too Young," and I told David about my day in the Basque restaurant: none of the customers had sworn at me; I hadn't dropped anything; Mrs.

Etcheverria called me her little *maketua,* which meant out-
sider, or non-Basque.

David talked about his brothers, about how Lloyd used
to give him his socks. "Socks?" I asked, and David said,
"Yes, I was the youngest and I was end of the line for
clothes; my socks always had holes."

"I mean," he added, "Mom tried to darn them, and all
that." He looked sad, but maybe that was the effect of the
coffee-shop lights, blue ones recessed into a star-pocked
ceiling. He started talking about his father.

David's father had died of a broken neck. "He fell in the
gully; he was drunk." And I remembered that I had known
this and I wanted to hold David's hand, but didn't do it.
Jen came back with a bottle of wine. "Our mixed special,
the heels of six leftover bottles; move over and let grandma
sit down." Jen was about twenty-six and had bleached
hair, which she piled on top of her head.

She made both of us feel better because she was cheerful
and uninvolved; she talked about growing up in Winnemucca and wanting to marry an Indian, and we talked
about growing up in French Ford, both of us carefully not
giving the town a name.

Walking home with David afterwards, I looked at the
bare, swept-clean sidewalks, at the wooden houses with
their scrawny trees and at the bank of blue-black mountains, and suddenly I wanted to tell David about Steve,
about Steve and Indiana, about how it had ended for me.

David walked close; I started talking and the story came
out fast—the week in San Francisco, the interview in the
Mark Hopkins, the lights going out, and finally me, the
next morning, on the bus going to Reno.

"What do you mean," David said when I had stopped talking, "he didn't do it to you?"

"It was to Indy."

"To you. And to everybody else he knew. But, especially you."

I said, "Oh God, David."

David said, "To Indiana. To you. To Phil. To your dad." We walked on for a while. The snow had been piled at the sides of the road; the clean sidewalk was marked by glassy patches. David kicked one of these ice slicks; it came loose in a sheet. "All the while he was engaged to you he was screwing her."

I clutched my stomach. I wanted to sit down on the frozen sidewalk and put my head on my knees.

David said, "He must have hated himself."

Across the dark, clean Winnemucca street was superimposed another picture: the time Steve and I walked down Deep Creek Road to see Lenny Barr and the cats. It had been a brilliant blue and white day and I had packed us a lunch of pâté sandwiches; I was wearing a skimpy purple dress with orange California poppies on it. When we got to the bottom of Deep Creek Road the river and its bed were spread out before us, churning and glinting gray and white with flashes of gold. And Steve stood beside it and said, "I look out of my eyes and I don't see anything; it's all darkness; it's staring into the pit."

Now, I thought, walking with David on the windy street, I understand why Steve pulled back when he began to get close to me, why he held me and then lost it: he was afraid of me looking into him, that would have been the worst of all, because I partially understood. And he was

179

afraid of being afraid, and afraid that I was good. And afraid that he would do it again. I thought about being afraid that I was good and said out loud, "A lot he knew."

"He did know a lot," David said. "Were you ever with him when he got started talking? Late at night?"

"Lots and lots." We kept on walking, side by side, but not touching.

I wanted to say, David, you've helped me a lot. It was in some ways one of my best evenings with David, and in some other ways one of the worst.

19

David and I stood on Lookout Trail and stared down at Winnemucca. "It looks like a company town," he said.

"Maybe railroad." The railroad track traced its insect pattern across the sandy flats patched with snow. Parallel with the railroad was the highway. That big shape on the edge of town was the casino; the bubble attached to it was the glass cover of the swimming pool. It was fed by a hot spring; steam came up on both sides of the glass dome.

It was Monday, a day off for both of us. Jen had loaned us her car and a map of the trails and gravel roads; she had told David about another hot spring partway up the mountain.

The day was crisp and bright; it felt good to be out. David had a thermos of coffee in his overcoat pocket. We walked on the wide trail; a bluejay squawked from a tree and threw inch-long pine cones. I said, "Evva says Daddy's been looking for me."

I went on. "It made me feel funny: bad, guilty, to hear

about Daddy. He hired a detective in Sacramento because that's where I made Evva say I was. And I'm here."

We were climbing, hugging the side of the hill. Part of the trail was snow-covered; there were some ice patches and some stretches of melted mud where underground hot water had leaked across the path. David said, "Did I tell you I knew your father?"

I said, "No," cautiously. Everyone in French Ford knew Daddy.

"First he knew me, and then he knew my mother. Remember when he came to the school to talk about county history?"

My father did that every year. "Yes."

"Well, I went up after class and told him about some stuff I had found in the yard. Some Chinese pottery."

There had been a Chinese settlement in French Ford during the Gold Rush.

"And then I asked him if he thought the McCrackens might be part Chinese, and he said maybe."

I looked at David and saw that this was a possibility. The set of the eyes and the cheekbones might be Chinese.

"Your father asked me if I wanted to be Chinese, and I said I did."

"Why?"

"I don't know. Partly, it seemed romantic. And partly because of the way they'd been treated. I always went with the underdog.

"He talked to me a long time. I was only eight, and he took me seriously. When he said goodbye he said, 'If there's anything I can help you with, let me know.'

"So when Mom took me to Dogtown I told her about him. He was the one got me into Friends' School."

We walked for a while longer. I said, "I like that story a lot."

At the next bend we sat on a rock and drank coffee and stared at the town, smaller now, its slanted tin roofs glittering crazily, the huddled white wooden buildings sad in their protective rows. Being above them felt powerful. The steam came out from the swimming pool only on one side of the building, like a huge leak.

The country around Winnemucca was either dusty tan, over and over, tan stone scoured by some long-ago weather, or white if there was snow on it. The rock we were sitting on was this same powdery tan, with snow in its crevices; behind us rose a tan guttered wall, trees growing out of it at sharp angles.

"What will happen with the House Un-American Activities Committee?" I asked.

David moved his shoulders. "Someone will get famous."

I imagined Steve making a sentimental speech, a get-famous speech about the American Way and the Meaning of Freedom. There was a citizens' committee attached to the Un-American Committee; it was called Save America. Steve could make speeches about them; he could be cynical and righteous: "*Save* America; America isn't saved? The struggle of our parents and grandparents, our forefathers, our Declaration of Independence, our hundreds of years of fighting for right and justice; *those* didn't save America?" Or perhaps he could be ironic and go on about saving things: string, paper bags, postage stamps, America . . .

"Maybe he won't be that kind," David said. "Maybe he'll be one of the others."

"One of the un-Americans?"

183

David said, "Maybe," and I said, "Oh God." I could see that that was possible, too.

"I think the hot spring is around the bend," David told me after a while.

The hot spring was a pond in a rock basin. The rock was gray and the pond gray and yellow, with a blue crust around its uneven edge. Clots of bubbles grew in the bottom of the water and rose to the surface and popped. We sat down and finished the coffee and warmed our hands over the steam from the pond. I said, "This is almost as good as French Ford."

"I have a surprise for us." David reached into his overcoat pocket. "I bought each of us a cake with blue icing." The blue icing on the cakes was almost the same color as the crust on the edge of the pond. I held my cake down to compare, and the colors matched.

"Watch out," David said, "it'll pick up the taste."

He was right; the cake tasted brackish, but I ate it anyway. "I like it this way," I told him.

The various uncertainties in our lives seemed to make an electricity around us that other people found attractive.

Perhaps we gave off a static like the current under the P G and E pylon. I felt we did.

"You kids are so sweet together."

"I'm going to embroider that on a sampler," I told David.

He was literal. "Do you embroider?"

"No." The Proffits, the people who drank and dropped things, had invited us for an evening in their room. I dressed up for this occasion. Mrs. Proffit had made it clear that it was a party, even though it only involved walking down the hall and into a bedroom that was pink instead of aqua.

"How can anybody, any couple, their age, live in a *rooming* house?" I was wearing my black sweater and skirt. Neither of us had much of a wardrobe.

The minute I said this I saw it was a Dowell remark. "Never mind, I'm sorry."

David said mildly, "All it takes is a couple of bad breaks." He took my hand and we walked down the hall to the Proffits' room.

"Here they are," Mrs. Sanchez greeted us. "The darlings." She fluffed up my hair.

We sat in chairs and Mrs. Sanchez and the Proffits sat on the bed. Mr. Dodd brought his own chair up from downstairs.

He reminded me of Lenny Barr. He was small and stocky and bowlegged, with a round, handsome, black-browed face. He had found the chair on a junk pile. "A real good chair. I fixed it up *right*. Anytime you want anything fixed, you little McCrackens, just let me know."

It was a nice party, except for the time when Mr. Dodd talked about guns and how every man should have one, and Mrs. Sanchez told him that was dangerous. "Mr. Dodd, you do that, and before you know it somebody gets *shot*."

Mr. Dodd said any ex-soldier knew that with a gun in his hand he was a man again.

"You're scaring our young couple." Mrs. Proffit had been watching me. She was a nice-looking woman, except that her face and hands were swollen, as if they had been under water. She had drunk a lot tonight, but the only sign of it was that her speech got slower.

The Etcheverrias also invited us out. They had a house halfway up the side of the mountain; you had to go there in a Jeep. We looked at the view and ate steak. "Seems like we get enough Basque food on the job," Mrs. E. said. "Do you like it?"

I said I did and she sighed and said, "You get tired. It's nice having a *maketua* around. I get tired of the *Euskaldunak*."

"Hey," Mr. E. told her. "Think it. Don't say it." *Euskaldunak*, he explained, was the Basque people.

"She doesn't really mean it," he added.

David asked questions, and we talked about Basque separatism, which was complicated and went far back in history. Mr. E. looked concentrated and somber when he explained the Basque cause.

Their house was made of rock, with redwood timbers and an overhanging red tile roof; they said it was copied from houses in the Pyrenees, the mountains that run between France and Spain.

"We built the house ourselves," Mr. Etcheverria said. "We hauled the redwood trees," he spread his arms to indicate their size, "from your state, from California."

Both the Etcheverrias had been born in Nevada. They didn't have accents, but there was something different about their speech.

I liked the dark floors in the house, and the red-striped rugs.

"*They* certainly have something they believe in," I said to David later that night.

"Do you know what Emma Goldman said?" he asked

me. "There are no races and no special causes; all issues are one issue, the fight of human beings for their fair share."

I looked at David and thought about the Dowell Socialism. I had always liked the idea of that Socialism, but it hadn't ever seemed very real to me before this.

Thanksgiving at Etcheverria's Restaurant was a pleasant family-style event. There was a turkey, and homemade ice cream, and the customers sang songs in Basque. These weren't Thanksgiving songs; they were songs about Our Homeland. "The Basques are angry at both the French and the Spanish," Mrs. Etcheverria said. "These songs are against the Spanish. Take this dish of cranberry sauce out there, please, darling."

Thanksgiving at the Bob Cat meant that David and I had lobster every night for four nights. Everyone in the gourmet restaurant wanted turkey, not lobster, so there was lots of leftover lobster for Jen to give us. And on Thanksgiving night the other customers in the café were very drunk.

Jen was cross as she slipped our platters down. "Fighting off that bunch of apes. Jeez Christ. You need six arms." To David she said, "Did you see Nicky?" Nicky was the manager. "If Nicky doesn't like this he can fire me."

She sat down with us and pulled a crumpled cigarette from under her belt. "Jeez Christ," she tinkered with the extended tobacco shreds, "it's bad enough now, you should see this place at Christmas. A zoo." David lit her cigarette. "So, how are you lovebirds?"

I let David answer while I sat sideways with my back against the wall of the booth and thought about Thanksgiving. Partly I was homesick and partly I wasn't.

Thanksgiving in French Ford had always been a big event. Daddy didn't usually serve turkey; he cooked pheasant or goose or guinea hen. One year he had suggested venison; he had planned so long for this venison and had found so many recipes that it was difficult for me to talk him out of it. "You eat beef," he told me, "so why not deer; the animal does not suffer at all; death is instantaneous," and "Hey, baby, maybe you'd better stop wearing shoes if it means so much to you, not killing creatures with pretty brown eyes."

It wasn't until Sybil suggested a buffalo roast that Daddy agreed to change his mind. The buffalo had belonged to a government herd, and Daddy could get it through the university's agricultural school.

"Your father takes delight in an idea," Sybil said. "It becomes an object in itself."

"You're the one who does that. He's just stubborn."

"Oh, no." Her laugh made me feel that she had some special, powerful secret.

We were washing the Minton china for the Thanksgiving dinner. This china, with its knobs and curlicues and gold-painted valleys, collected dust during the months when it wasn't being used.

"Do you think," I said, "that that stubbornness of Daddy's is why he hasn't married again?" I was twelve years old and was interested in psychological questions.

Sybil said, "He is *un*realisitic," and Mrs. Farmer, from the stove, said, "Grace, you just stop that."

"Everyone says it's because he's so crazy about me," I went on. "But I know that's not why."

Sybil said, "Probably not."

She smiled at a gold-bordered bowl with violets painted in the hollow where the soup would go. "Of course there have been people," she said. "Women. Lots of them."

"Of course." I wondered who they might have been.

"But something always happens . . . We Dowells," Sybil said, after thinking about it for a minute, "are much too romantic."

Romantic, I thought, and dried a lacy plate on a red-checked dishtowel. That didn't seem exactly right, either.

I watched my father during dinner. He wore his Navy Medical Corps uniform, dark blue jacket with gold-striped sleeves. He stood up to slice the buffalo roast, which had been soaked in red wine and cooked with shallots, basil, and carrot. ("And just a tough cow, all the same," Mrs. Farmer said.) Daddy's eyes shone; alert and pleased, he presided over his domain of white tablecloth, silver tureen and platters, relatives ranged along the sides of the table, his household of people, all female. The table that year included me, Sybil, Indiana, and Mrs. Farmer, who ate with us on holidays.

In books, widowers married their housekeepers and it did not matter that the housekeeper was old and grand-motherly; that was what the widower wanted. I watched Mrs. Farmer and thought about this and finally rejected it. Then I turned to Indiana. Indiana seemed more of a possibility even though she was only seventeen. But I eventually rejected Indiana, too. Daddy was carving more buffalo roast; his thinning hair flopped vulnerably and sweetly.

There was wild rice and gooseberry jam to go with the roast. It seemed clear that what Daddy really wanted was to sit at the head of this table and serve meals like this one.

Jen ground her cigarette out on the rim of David's plate. "I could get you more lobster, but by now you'd prolly puke at just the idea."

She looked tired and one panel of her blonde beehive had started to sag. I tucked it up for her.

I remembered how my father used to pat my hair and joke about its styling. Maybe Daddy had been shy. Maybe he was afraid to tell me he loved me in any way except the protective, "You're my girl, baby. My girl, of course. How'd you make the coiffure do that today?" Pat, pat.

I missed my father. I thought of his face, with its arrogant nose and cheerful insecure eyes. I had been unfair to him. I wanted to telephone him.

"It was really nice of you to get us the lobster," I said to Jen. "Thanks a lot."

20

When you are especially interested in a subject everything will conspire to remind you of it.

On the way home from the Bob Cat Coffee Shop three men in the street looked like Daddy. Mrs. Sanchez met us at the door with a story about Mrs. Proffit calling home and learning that her father had had a stroke.

I got undressed and climbed into bed with the paper. "David. I'm worried about Daddy."

He was reading *Red Star Over China*. "Just a sec."

I went back to my newspaper. There was a story about a man who was arrested for stealing a Thanksgiving turkey for his family.

"I have to call him. I have to call my father."

"What?" He pulled himself loose from his book. "It's eleven-thirty."

I had begun to get dressed. "I have to."

David didn't say anything about the possible danger to him of a phone call to French Ford. "It's cold out. Wear the gloves." We had only one pair between us.

I called from the phone booth at the Texaco station.

I had remembered Evva's schedule and thought she would be working tonight. When she learned what I wanted she was very angry. "Talk about nerve. Honest to God, Grace."

"You can if you want to. Please. Evva, you said you'd help me."

Finally she agreed to put a phone call through to Daddy and pretend it came from Sacramento.

"Christ, Grace." She clunked buttons.

There was some buzzing and snapping, cold noises coming out of the receiver while I scraped my feet back and forth to keep the circulation going.

And, after a while, my father's voice.

"Daddy? Daddy, it's Grace."

He said, "Grace." Then he said, "Oh, honey."

I could see him exactly, the eager, active face, the bags under the eyes, the shoulder-sag that happened when he thought he wasn't being watched. "Honey, what happened?"

"It wasn't your fault."

"Yes, baby, but what happened? You were scared. I pushed you. Into marrying Steve."

"I miss you so."

"Tell me why you went away."

"I'm sorry, I'm sorry."

Finally I said, "It wasn't anything you did; Steve did something; I can't tell you what; you didn't do anything, nothing, I just have to stay away for a while."

I said, "Listen, I miss you; tell me what you're wearing."

"What I'm wearing, baby?"

"Yes. Is it your blue pants? Gray wool shirt?"

192

"What I'm *wearing*."

"Brown leather loafers?"

Daddy, I'll come back pretty soon, really I will, and when I do it will be all right and, really, Daddy, it is okay, I am forgetting about Steve; pretty soon I'll be able to be in a place where Steve might come and not be sick to my stomach . . .

I didn't say any of this; I said, "Tell me about the Placer Historical Society."

"I haven't been doing much . . ."

"Bird-watching? Stamps?"

"Not at the moment. You see, baby . . ."

"Has it snowed yet?"

"Almost. Yesterday."

"Daddy, I keep thinking about that party. The one for Sybil."

"Hey, baby, I'm sorry about that."

"No. It was a *great* party. I keep thinking about your pâté."

"Well, *hey* now." He sounded pleased. Now was the time to conclude this conversation. Tell him I'm fine. I'll be home soon. Don't worry. I'm fine, *really*. Instead, I said, "God, Daddy, I missed you," and heard myself make a gutsy sob, halfway up the throat, the kind that sounds like a belch but is recognizable, emotional. *What are you doing sobbing into my pâté?* Grace, maybe all this time you've been maligning your father. Maybe he's the one who really feels things and you're the one who fobs them off with the clever don't-tell-me. And you had, whatchamacallit, *attributed . . .*

"How's Sybil?"

"Fine. I mean, okay. Of course, she's not . . ."

"And Mrs Farmer?"

"Oh. Fine."

And so on. And so on. And eventually it trickled away, at least some of it, and I said, "Daddy, Daddy, I love you," and lied about my being in Sacramento, and invented weather for Sacramento and told him about that, and kissed him twice, telephone kisses, smack, smack, And then I hung up.

I came out of the phone booth and David was waiting for me. I had left him in our room at Mrs. Sanchez's, lying on the floor with a chair cushion behind his head, reading *Red Star,* making pencil marks in the margin. He had said, "Hey, good luck," when I left the room, but he hadn't seemed very concerned.

And here he was, leaning against the wall of the darkened Texaco station, hands in pockets, an arc light sputtering over his head. He was kicking one foot against the base of the wall to keep warm.

I wasn't sure at first who he was, and jumped back, startled. Then I said, "David. You came after me."

He moved under the streetlight, and I noticed, as if they were new to me, the curled eyelashes, the tight-pored skin, the blush across the cheekbones, all suddenly brightened by the overhead lamp. He smiled. "It's okay, then."

I said, "Oh, David, thank you," and reached up. His blue canvas coat was nubby and crisp, his face frosty, his breath, in its white cloud, warmly familiar, like the smell of a favorite blanket. The arc light snapped and sent off a blue spark; the wires hummed; the blue sparks descended between us, separating, dying into white comets. The arc light buzzed, a brooding electrical noise. David and I were set off by the glow and the mechanical sounds.

David reached down; I reached up.

194

The electricity made a loop around our heads and shoulders, a loop around our hips. David said, "I'm glad."

"Me too."

"I'm glad it came out all right."

"Yes."

"Do you want to celebrate?"

"Celebrate?" Nothing was open at night in Winnemucca except the Bob Cat.

"I've got the key to the swimming pool. Jen got it for me."

We had never been swimming in the Bob Cat's mineral pool because employees were allowed there only during dinner hour, when we were working. The pool was closed now.

I put my hand in his pocket. "Let's go." On the other side of the pocket, inside David's body, I felt a throbbing blood vessel; was it called the femoral vessel, the one that went down into your hip? "Okay, let's go."

David had three keys for the swimming pool.

The first was big, old-fashioned, hand-chased; a key to Castle Perilous. It unlocked a cleverly latticed iron gate. Then came key No. 2, small, brass, and door No. 2, opening onto a hall and empty reception desk, eerie in David's flashlight beam. And finally there was a third door, the kind that gives with a whoosh and is reinforced with metal.

Inside, moonlight shone through the glass dome and an icing of snow pressed against the steamy glass seams. At floor level the black swimming pool, disturbed by our door-opening, slapped its sides. It smelled of chlorine; fog rose in curls and wisps.

David and I circled the pool, walking carefully.

195

Suddenly I couldn't stand my coat, scarf, gloves. I tugged at buttons and boot strings. I glanced sidelong at David. He was taking off his shirt. I decided not to look again, but just to go ahead, forward, forward! I peeled off bra, garter belt, stockings, probably snagging them, dropped everything in a heap. Leaving a clot of clothes behind me on the tiles, I jumped feet first into the water.

Below, ghostly, shone the rest of blue-white me. A bubble chased up my thigh and between my breasts. The water was warm and felt chalky, a tiny gritty resistance to thumb and forefinger.

David performed an elegant, professionally arced dive and swam the length of the pool.

Down at the end, I could see him only as an occasional flash of white heralded by the slap of water. Then he passed me, with almost no splashing, elbows in. "You'll never be a good swimmer," they had told me at Colfax Pool, "too bony, no control." David had control.

Eight times up and down the pool. I counted them. He looked beautiful.

Finally he pulled up beside me. I said, "Hello, hotshot."

He shook his head to get the water out of his eyes. Then he put his arms around me and kissed me.

Neither of us had any clothes on and David had an erection.

I thought, so this is the way it goes.

The two months of debate and stopgap were not going to matter. We pulled ourselves out of the water.

I thought, there's heat under these tiles. They were warm and grainy; my thigh fitted nicely onto them. I turned toward David and lay down. I said it aloud. "Everything's going to be wonderful."

A slide-show picture moved across my brain: an Aztec woman was jumping off the steps of a pyramid; below her gray-green water waited; above her was a harsh blue sky.

A triangle of heat formed across my belly, down between my legs. Something turned over inside me, a small valve or mouth opened and extended itself in an oval. David's hand moved over my belly, flat fingers with pulses in them.

I wanted to tell him I loved him, but I was afraid to say that. Maybe it wasn't true.

I told him again, "Everything's going to be wonderful."

21

"Hey," Jen said, "what happened to you two babies; did you discover plutonium?"

She slid into the booth beside me. "You've got *That Look*. Like you won the Irish sweeps."

David had good control. He smiled politely. I was afraid I was blushing.

Jen poked me in the ribs. "If you learn any new ways; you know; any new how-tos; pass them on. You never know. Maybe I'll meet another guy some day."

I was pleased to discover that IT showed. Evva and I had talked about this, and Evva had said, no, it didn't show; nobody knew on the days when she and Lloyd had made love.

I hadn't told Evva that I thought her love didn't show because she and Lloyd weren't driven by True Love, but only by expediency. For me it would be True Love, and it was going to shine out like the Dowells' idea of God: haze around a street lamp.

"Why did they come to French Ford," I had asked Steve about the Dowells, "why not Chico?" and Steve said, "Aah, I hate them; they left so fucking much to live up to."

We had been lying on the cliff above the Quarry Pit; two hundred feet below us the pool shone chalky green in its nest of clay and pebbles. Steve gestured. "They did all this. All their wretched Utopian nonsense and they wrecked the landscape for the next hundred years."

I hadn't thought of the diggings that way, but of course it was true. The hydraulic mining that the Dowells financed had scoured the ground so clean nothing grew there.

I remembered this now, in Winnemucca, and thought: "David grew there." The phrase marched into my head emblazoned and embellished and decorated, like what I'd been saying about embroidering something on a sampler.

I had started phoning David during the day at work. I was calling him on the Bob Cat's house phone to tell him what had happened during the last hour. I did this so often that Jen said, "Hey Grace, you better cut down on that. Any more and you'll get him fired."

"David, don't leave me," I said that night.

"Huh?"

David was behind me in the bed, bony and reassuring, warm belly pressed into my back; hands cupping my stomach. I said, "I love it when you hold me like that."

I didn't add, Don't get taken away from me, don't get arrested, but I suppose both of us thought that. I started talking to him about Steve and me in the graveyard.

"Are you saying," David asked, "that he would get part of the way into making love to you and then stop?"

"He only did that once."

I waited for David to offer an explanation of Steve's

behavior. David raised himself up from the bed and stared at me. Then he began to kiss me, slowly and gently, moving down my body from the collarbone.

I had been keeping a journal in which I wrote down my dreams about Steve.

I remembered that Evva's psychiatry book had said a journal was "a way of managing the emotions."

Steve and I have had a hydrocephalic child. Steve is nice to this child, the way he was with some of the old men at the District Office . . .

Steve is driving a snow-removal machine. He reverses it, fast, toward me, staring at the controls, not looking at me. I run to escape him; I wake up.

Steve is a ticket-taker on a dark, clanking nighttime train. I'm the only passenger . . .

One day when David had to work late I came home and took the dream journal into the bathroom and tore the pages out one by one and flushed them down the toilet.

I had almost stopped having these dreams. And the last time I had one I didn't know in the dream who Steve was. I looked at him, and at one level recognized him, and at another said, who is that man, why am I watching him?

David turned over and pressed his body against mine. After a while he said, "*Grace* means 'effortless beauty or charm.' I looked it up in the dictionary."

He added, "It also means 'temporary immunity from a deadline.'" He kissed me and then we made love so energetically and possessively that all the covers ended up on the floor. As I pushed against David I said, "No deadline, David; no deadline, David; no deadline ever."

* * *

"Hi," Mrs. Sanchez said, "There is a *lady* waiting to see you."

The way she said Lady, with a capital L, made me suspicious; it couldn't be Jen, who would be referred to as a girl, nor Evva, also a girl; it seemed unlikely that it could be . . .

I went toward Mrs. Sanchez's front room, upholstered in wine-colored velour, around the curve of the archway, and there, indeed, sitting on the wine-colored overstuffed couch, was the Lady, wearing her pink tweed suit and her ground-gripper shoes, which were placed side by side on Mrs. Sanchez's country-cottage tweed rug. Sybil sat erect with her shoulders as far back as she could get them; her spine was as always still cramped in its old lady's curve.

She stared at me. "I had a difficult time finding you."

I bent to kiss her, but she turned her face away. "Emotion is not enough, Grace; that has always been the problem in our family, too much emotion and too little feeling; your friend Evva claims you are getting married again."

I sat on the couch and took her hand; she let it lie limp in mine. I resisted saying that Evva couldn't possibly have told her any such thing.

"Not that I object. I myself have been married five times." She stared reprovingly at a corner of the fireplace.

I corrected her: "Four times. That's what you've always said."

I got the impression that Sybil really remembered that it was four, not five.

"I am happy to see you," she added appraisingly. "I arrived on the Greyhound bus. It was an interesting trip. A man was abusive and had to be helped off the bus. In a town named Edge. I would not have liked to spend time there."

"It was nice of you to come, Aunt Sybil."

She continued to frown. "I do not see how you could *think* of getting married without me."

I put my arms around her, and after a few minutes she leaned against me. I stroked her ear and cheek.

"It is all in the mind, of course, Grace. You can be happily married under any circumstances. You can be happily married to anybody."

"Yes, naturally I remember you," Sybil told David. "You are the one who looks like my last husband; he was nice."

Mrs. Sanchez said that Sybil could stay in the room in the basement. "I hate to offer her that; she's such an elegant lady. Breeding, Grace; it shows; it's nice to know about."

I didn't tell Mrs. Sanchez that Sybil usually lived in the back seat of a car. Sybil had arrived without any luggage. I explained that she was used to having people do things for her; if there was no one to pack her bags she simply left without them. Mrs. Sanchez agreed. "Yes, one can see all that."

"I have come to help them get married," Sybil explained to Mrs. Sanchez. "My niece has been dilatory. About getting married."

"Dilatory?" Mrs. Sanchez's voice went high.

"I am glad to be here to help her." Sybil followed Mrs. Sanchez into the basement room. "Marriage as an institution certainly is demanding," she said.

Mrs. Sanchez repeated, "Demanding." This time she sounded more reflective than panicky.

202

I was listening at the top of the basement stairs, and I thought, *oh-oh.*

The next morning Mrs. Sanchez was waiting for David and me when we got up. "Grace," she said, separating me off from him when we appeared in the downstairs hall, "Now, could I perhaps speak to you?"

She batted the sparse mascara'd lashes and pulled a smile across her plump painted face. I gestured to David and she patted me ahead of her into the dining room.

Mrs. Sanchez's dining room spoke to me, more than any of the other alien places I had been seeing, of a life different from my own past. It was strange that other settings, much more eccentric than this high, dark-stained veneered sideboard and table, did not give me the feeling that, suddenly, I understood all the people in the world who had never lived in French Ford with Daddy and Sybil and the ghosts of all the Dowells.

"Now," Mrs. Sanchez said, "now," and made her eyelashes quiver.

I was expecting the speech that followed and picked up only occasional phrases: "found it hard to believe . . . am sure you didn't understand . . . dear children, really . . . your lovely aunt . . ."

At this point I said, "Excuse me, Mrs. Sanchez," and went out and pulled David in from the hall, where he was reading the *Winnemucca Register.* "She wants us to get married," I told him.

He and I sat on one side of the table and Mrs. Sanchez sat on the other. It was like being in court, I thought.

I wished she would stop smiling. The heart-shaped face and spiked eyelashes were threatening, somehow.

"So," she concluded, "and such a sweet couple. But since your auntie says you are getting married. I love to see

203

a lovely young couple . . . It will have to be soon, though." She rose and moved, smiling like Mona Lisa, into her kitchen. David and I stared at each other.

"She thinks she can force us."

"With that smug, sweet smile."

"Let's go upstairs."

In our room, David climbed on the bed and stacked the pillows behind him; I sat in the chair and chewed on my fingernail corners. After a while Sybil came in. "I do not understand." She fitted herself, in a gingerly way, onto a bed corner. "Don't you want to get married?"

We looked at each other. "We don't want to be forced to."

"But I have been forced into many things. I have been forced to get old."

David and I exchanged glances again. "That's not the same thing, Aunt Sybil." David had started calling Sybil "Aunt" as soon as she arrived. He said that he had to call her something. And Sybil, all by itself, did not seem respectful.

"It is *exactly* the same thing. Getting old and getting married are both major life changes. And both . . . what is the word? Pose? Suppose?"

"Posit?"

"Yes. Posit. Both posit a force stronger than oneself. A force that is working on one."

David said he didn't like Mrs. Sanchez being the force stronger than himself, and Sybil said it was not Mrs. Sanchez, it was Society. I said I could not get married without my father. It would break his heart; he had been excited about my marriage. He had had elaborate plans for it.

There was a silence while we thought. "He wanted you to march through French Ford," Sybil remembered.

"Yes."

"He had read about that in the *National Geographic*."

I began to shred my paper handkerchief and make a neat pile of the scraps.

"If you were married here," Sybil said, "it would be a civil ceremony only. A legal formality. Not a ritual."

"It's still getting married."

"It's all in the mind." She peered at me hopefully. "In France, everyone is married twice. One civil marriage, one religious."

"Not if they're not religious."

"Everyone."

I was contemplating Daddy's procession through French Ford. Probably France was correct; France was the country that had given him that idea.

I raised my eyes to find David watching me. "Grace?"

I answered him by looking at him.

"How about it?"

"How about *what?*" (*It.* I knew what he meant. The all-purpose word, *it.*)

He climbed off the bed and came to sit on the arm of the chair. He looked graceful, poised, and scared. A warm hand reached out and took mine and examined it, first the palm and then the back. Sybil belched mildly. "I think he is going to propose to you."

"Grace," Sybil said after a minute, "David is, I think, going to propose."

It should have been a ridiculous moment, with Sybil egging us on. But it wasn't.

David said, "Grace, will you marry me?"

I said, "Yes. Yes, David, I will."

22

"Although it is only a civil ceremony," Sybil said, "it is important that it be done right."

"I feel guilty about Daddy."

"Something you neglect to consider, Grace, is that *I* am old. I will not be here permanently. If you are to be married in my lifetime you should do it now."

I read the ads over Sybil's shoulder. "I don't like the ones that have two bells and a length of ribbon."

Sybil didn't like the ones with mottos. " 'For the Tie That Binds.' That is threatening."

She decided finally that she approved of Saylor's Chapel. "The ad is large and quiet. It is genteel."

We were sitting in Mrs. Sanchez's dining room next to the mahogany veneer sideboard. Mrs. Sanchez had invited Sybil to use the dining room anytime she wanted.

"Aunt Sybil," I said, "you will live forever."

"Oh, I don't think so." She studied the ad with appreciation. "This one will do nicely. One wants it, of course. To live forever. It is difficult to admit the existence of other possibilities. I wonder about it sometimes."

"How is my father?" I realized with surprise that I hadn't asked her about this yet.

"The same." She turned the page from *Weddings* to *Welding*. "*Welding* is a strange word." She repeated it, moving her lips experimentally. "*Welding*."

Sybil was in a perfectly sane mood this week, saner than most people. She offered practical questions about licenses and birth certificates; she asked us to buy her a suit. "I will repay you when I return. I cannot go to your wedding in my pink; I have worn it on the Greyhound bus."

Maybe her interest in the wedding had kicked her forward into sanity. I'd heard of things like that happening.

Saylor's Chapel was a sizable building with a glass front. It was on Route 40, at the opposite end of town from the Bob Cat.

Saylor's was not just a wedding chapel, it was a burial chapel, too. Its neat anonymous architecture, unstressed and bland, stretched out along the highway, ready for any function. "All things to any person," I whispered to David, who looked as if he might understand.

Jen parked her Ford convertible by the dove-colored awning, and David and I, hands tightly interlocked, climbed out. The chapel's Mr. Saylor wore a blue-gray suit to match his blue-gray rug; Mrs. Saylor had blue hair. I was in white—a white knit dress—Sybil had insisted: "I know what is right, Grace; you are not to wear yellow; rose would not be so bad. But you are a Virgin Bride."

Jen wore emerald green, Sybil her new gray tweed, David a dark suit, Mrs. Sanchez, included because Sybil had said, "I have grown fond of that lady," was fluffed out in pink angora. As we drifted colorfully past our plate glass reflections Mrs. Saylor handed out camellias. David whispered, "I'm terrified."

"Me, too."

"Dearly beloved . . ."

I resented that Mr. Saylor should say *Dearly Beloved,* which was the minister's line. Mr. Saylor was not a minister. "By and through the authority vested in me by the State of Nevada . . ."

Mrs. Saylor played the organ. She had asked me what music I wanted. "Down on the Levee" was the only song I could remember the name of. "Surely," she said, " 'Oh, Promise Me'?" And I told her no, firmly enough that she went over to the organ and started batting out, with both hands and both feet, "Roses Love Sunshine," not badly at all.

I couldn't hear the service for wondering what really would have been my preferred wedding song if I had had time to think about it. Nothing came except the French Ford school song and the Triumphal March from *Aïda.* "Down on the Levee" went on and on. What were some of those other words? "Build me a castle, ninety feet high/So I can see her/As she rides by." Sad words, certainly, and the love affair they talked about must be ending sadly.

I was thinking about this when Mr. Saylor asked me, did I take David to be and so forth, and I heard my voice saying *I do.* Then I stared down at my feet.

"You can dye them afterwards," Sybil had said about the white shoes. "You *have* to have white. I won't live long."

David said, "I do," and Mr. Saylor told us to kiss.

208

"David," I whispered, "it doesn't seem real," and he nodded and then, underwater, none of the sensations getting through, my ears ringing, we touched lips. Mrs. Saylor banged hard at . . . I remembered the other words to that song, "Birmingham Jail": "Send me a letter/Send it by mail/Send it in care of/Birmingham Jail . . ." Why on earth did I do this?

"That is lovely; this is perfectly lovely," Sybil said, "it was a *perpetual* service." I thought, oh, my God, she's off again; *perpetual* is not the word she wants; what she wants is something like *perfect*, or *moving*, or *sincere*. The funeral parlor atmosphere has gotten to her. Sybil, hold my hand.

Crash, went Mrs. Saylor, locking the key on Birmingham Jail. Jen cried into a blue and green silk handkerchief.

Mr. Saylor said, "Young people, may I congratulate you from the bottom of my heart."

Mrs. Saylor got up from the organ bench, dusted off the front of her skirt, and came forward, arms extended. I thought she was going to embrace us, or at least me, but she had more complicated plans; she held her arms wide and high, like a referee indicating the winner of a prizefight; one wing of her blue-gray hair collapsed, a movable sculpture; she said, "I have the most marvelous surprise for you young people," and waved her arms at the glass doors.

About ten people came in through the doors. Some of these people had cameras and said, "Look this way, please; smile; hey, another little one; smile there, baby; my God; that's a pretty one." Some of the other people had ruled notepads with spiral bindings and said, "What do you think of this? How do you like it; are you thrilled?"

"What's happening, what have we done?" I asked. David said, "I don't know; I never got married before."

We both began to understand at about the same time that this wasn't simply part of the package; Saylor's didn't do this for everyone who got married in their funeral parlor. Someone finally explained: we were the ten thousandth couple. "Think of it," Mrs. Saylor said, "ten thousand, ten zero zero zero. All of those lovely lovely young people. Today certainly is your lucky day."

One of the reporters had a large white box tied with white satin ribbon. She opened this; it held a set of stainless steel cookware, every size from baby one-egg to Thanksgiving turkey, each with copper bottom and streamlined black plastic handle.

"Oh, my," Mrs. Saylor said, "this is certainly your lucky day."

"How does it feel to get married?" the Winnemucca reporter asked. He didn't listen to our answer, and wrote in his notebook, looking pleased.

After a while there was champagne. And quite a bit later we were back in Mrs. Sanchez's veneered dining room, Jen in her tight green faille, pink Mrs. Sanchez, the slightly drunken Proffits, the Etcheverrias. We sat around the dining table on the matching chairs. The table held a lace tablecloth and more champagne, a cake with people on it, five pottery candlesticks shaped like gnomes.

"I wanted it festive." Mrs. Sanchez moved the eyelashes. "Is it festive, dear?"

I thought of Daddy's dinner party. "It's lovely, Mrs. Sanchez. Thank you."

Mr. Dodd, whose name rhymed with God, arrived and

toasted us: "Wealth, health, and four beautiful kids." The Proffits each drank four glasses of champagne, one after the other. They leaned their elbows on the table and looked morose and flushed. Mr. Etcheverria sang a Basque wedding song.

And finally David and I were alone upstairs in our room with its polka dot curtains. He said, "I guess that really does it," and I answered, "Yes," and we fell asleep, too tired to make love.

The next morning the story was in both the *Winnemucca Register* and the *Reno Observer*.

The pictures were sweet. We smiled out in gray half-tone, happy, healthy, surprised, just the way the new couple is supposed to look. And we were clearly recognizable, dead on; nobody could possibly have thought that we were not us.

David crumpled the corner of the newspaper. "There it is," he said, and I said, yes. Maybe we'd better pack, he said; I said, Maybe. He said, Just me; really; it's just me.

I got angry at this. "We're married now."

Sybil came into the room and asked what we were doing. When we didn't answer she said, "If you're going somewhere I'm coming too."

We waited, Sybil curved and aggressive on the edge of the bed, a small hawk, David leaning against the dresser, I in the chair biting my fingernail corners. Suddenly I was sad about leaving Mrs. Sanchez's aqua room, where so many things had happened. "I like those blue polka dots," I said to David, and he agreed that he kind of liked them too.

"Where will we go?" Sybil asked. The curve of her spine

clenched into a C; she stared at her corded wrists. "I would like to go to French Ford." She thought about this. "*Near* French Ford."

"I feel at home there," she added, pulling at the skin of her wrist. "If you hold it tight," she exhibited the wrist, "it stays that way. It stays up when you pull on it."

I said, "I've always wanted to live for a while in Dogtown. We'll go to Dogtown."

And, I thought, if something happens, I can get home. If we're in Dogtown I can get home to Daddy if he needs me.

23

Sybil bought us a car.

I don't mean that Sybil paid for the car. She claimed she was doing so; the car would be our wedding present from her after she got back to French Ford and got her money. But David and I didn't count on this.

We gave her three hundred dollars from our savings and from the Etcheverrias' wedding present, we put this in her purse and walked her to the edge of the used-car lot.

"Pray," David said, watching her round the corner, hunched in her black felt coat, black gloves, and new Salvation Army hat. "Just pray."

"She can be bright when she wants to," I told him hopefully.

She was back within the hour, slowly driving a fifteen-year-old black Packard whose headlights stuck high out of its fenders. She didn't have a driver's license, but no one had asked her about that.

"This is a nice car." She opened the door. "Perhaps I will live in it when all this is finished."

Sybil wasn't clear why we were to go to Dogtown, but she was pleased with the arrangement. "Dogtown will do very well for now. I have always wanted to explore Dogtown. This is a stopgap measure."

David and I knew it was a stopgap measure. We would live in Dogtown for three weeks, maybe four weeks, and something would change. Change was inherent in the situation.

Sybil sat on the far running board while we loaded the Packard with our suitcase and the aluminum pots and a cut-glass bowl from Mrs. Sanchez and the black silk sheets from Jen. Then there was my new copy of Proust and David's *Red Star*. Sybil would sit in the back, with the luggage. "Which is rather much, when it is really my car."

"It's a communally owned car." David put his arm around her. "It belongs to all of us; when you have moved out to the diggings we'll come and live with you."

At Reno we stopped to get gas and sandwiches and canned goods, and then we were heading back across the craggy scrubby mountains that separated California and Nevada. These mountains were gray and scaly while you were in Nevada and suddenly became Christmas-tree green after you had crossed the border. The car climbed well, and I leaned back and remembered riding this road with my head tucked against the bus window, crying.

We were going first to Comstock, across the diggings from French Ford. From there we would cross to Dogtown. Comstock and French Ford were only thirty-five miles apart, but no one in Comstock knew anybody in French Ford; the diggings made a barrier between the two towns. "Like the Great Wall of China," I said. "Like the line between BC and AD," David agreed. We told each other we were very witty.

There were five buildings in Dogtown.

The nicest of these was the Dogtown Bar, made of redwood logs, like a giant log cabin. It had no floor and no windows, but the bar still stood, with its polished redwood top and a set of shelves above. Hand-hammered black hinges showed where a low swinging door had gone out to the main room.

I walked around on the joists, touching things. The porcelain doorknobs on their black iron housing and the black, erratically shaped door hardware had been bolted down during the Gold Rush. They seemed magic objects that had made it safely out of the past without help.

That night we slept in the car, David and I in the front seat, Sybil in the back. I curled up with my head on David's lap, under the steering wheel. Sybil snored comfortingly: whistle, squeeze, whistle, squeeze. The velour car seat cupped my hip; David's legs under me and the steering wheel above made a safe enclosure. I have my family around me, I thought.

I awakened during the night with a jolt; something had thudded against the side of the car. I squeezed out from under the steering wheel; a blur outside the window, an animal head. A deer had run into us.

For a moment we stared at each other, the deer and I, she with bulging bright brown eyes fringed with long lashes; they looked like David's lashes. Then she veered off around the front of the car; she had been running away from something. Neither David nor Sybil woke up.

The next day David and I moved into the Dogtown Bar.

215

I scrubbed with David's undershirt; Mrs. Sanchez's cut-glass bowl went onto the redwood bar counter; our clothes were underneath. David got lumber from the last house down the road and began to fix the floor. The bowl should have looked ridiculous on the bar, but it didn't.

A large yellow house with a pine tree in front of it was next to the Dogtown Bar. Someone had been living in this house; it contained a cherry-wood chair and bed frame, some dishes, and a clean pot. The house was evenly coated with red dust; no one had lived there for a while. Still, I felt angry about the signs of possession.

The other three houses were strung out along the road that led into the diggings.

Sybil wanted the first house on the road: a two-room one, with all of its wood holding together, and the main room still papered in dark tan wallpaper with darker still roses.

"I wonder, did they used to be pink?" She scowled at the roses. "Someone should replace that paper. Still, there is a touch of—what would you say, Grace—innocence?"

I said, yes, that's right, innocence. The doors of Sybil's house had been painted white and were still almost white. She moved her new clothes from Winnemucca into the bedroom and I gave her our suitcase to use as a dresser. One of the auto seats would be a bed. Sunlight came dustily through the coated, small-paned windows. Maybe, I thought, this was Sybil's first house, ever. I was vague about those middle husbands.

In the evening we opened some of our cans and sat around a campfire and ate from them. I said, There is something permanent about a campfire, and Sybil said, What do you mean, permanent; it's completely unstable;

that is what makes it burn, and I said, No, as if the people around the fire are permanent, and Sybil said, Ah-ha, racial memory, and I said, Hypnosis.

David said, "Maybe we should tell stories."

"Tell us about Friends' School."

"I don't think I can tell stories about real things."

"Tell us about your first night there."

"I was thinking about the fire," Sybil said. "*What* are we talking about?"

David began: "When I was nine years old my mother brought me here to hide and after I had been here for a while she got me accepted into Friends' Settlement School. She came here and woke me up one night. She had brought soap and a damp washcloth. She washed my face and walked me out to Comstock."

"Washing your face was good," Sybil said, "if she was taking you to school."

"We got on the late bus," David said. "We reached Fairfield about two in the morning."

"And then what happened?"

"I don't remember. I was asleep; Mom said she handed me over to Ed like a package."

"Ed was the head of the school," I told Sybil.

David said, yes. "But I remember the next night. I felt glad to be there, but I wouldn't sleep in the bed. It was a nice bed, just an ordinary one, but I wouldn't sleep in it."

"You felt trapped."

"A commitment," said Sybil. "A bed is a commitment."

"Ed was wonderful about it. The other kids weren't superior or condescending, but they were kind of baffled. Here I was, new kid, silent, sulky, and I wouldn't sleep in a bed. He told them I was a pioneer boy. I'd been living in

217

the woods, living like a pioneer. 'Wildcats! Coyotes!' he said. He made it sound great. The other kids were really impressed. They were a little scared of me after that, but they liked me."

I lay down and put my head in David's lap. "Sybil, *you* tell a story."

Sybil waited only a minute. "I met my fifth husband in Foster's Cafeteria in San Francisco. He was the handsomest thing I had ever seen in my life; he had dark hair and dark eyes and a mustache and a hopeful, sweet *yearning* expression."

"What's a yearning expression?"

"Perhaps he was just hungry. I took my coffee cup over to his table and told him, 'I am feeling quite faint.' And a month after that we were married, and shortly thereafter I had one of my nervous breakdowns."

She paused. "I do not think the nervous breakdown was his fault. I still remember how beautiful he was."

Sybil told me, compressing her lips between the words, that pride goeth before a fall.

"What do you mean, Aunt Sybil?" It was the fourth day of our stay in Dogtown; it still hadn't snowed; the weather had remained dry and crisp, with brilliant sunlight patterning its way through the pine tree branches. Christmas was almost here. We sat on the warm splintered steps of Sybil's house; the world ended somewhere outside Dogtown.

"We are proud now," Sybil said, "we should beware."

I said, "Aunt Sybil, are you comfortable at night?" and she said, "I am perfectly warm enough. I am used to Living off the Land."

I said, "I think I'm falling in love with David."

Sybil said, "With whom? Oh, with your husband."

People become attached to possessions, too, I thought; maybe that caused as much trouble as loving people. I was getting fond of the Dogtown Bar, whose floor we had repaired; the Dogtown Bar and Sybil's house with the brown roses were ours, but so was the large house with the tree where someone had lived last summer; that was our house too, maybe we would move into it when the weather got hot again and the tree's shade was necessary. The other houses weren't ours but we had domain over them; no one else was supposed to live there.

"Do you think," I asked Sybil, "there is a destiny that shapes our ends, rough-hew them how we will?"

Sybil said, "No."

That was another thing that had been happening. I loved Sybil more now, the way I might have loved my mother if she had lived.

That night we sat around the campfire with a supper of canned beans and canned brown bread and I told the story of my job with Henry. "Ladies and gentlemen," I was reciting, "Our marvels of sexual excitation . . ." I was watching the trees behind the campfire as I said this, and among them, in the tree that shaded the house, I saw a glimmer of sinuous wobble; it was either a person or a big pale animal. I kept talking. "The marvels were in bottles or were stuffed. There was a two-headed snake and a two-headed calf and a five-legged chicken . . ." I let my voice trail off.

"What's the matter?" Sybil asked.

"There's somebody in that tree behind you." And at this point the person came out into the campfire light. After a

219

while Sybil said, "Hello," and I said, "Hello," because both Sybil and I knew the person. It was Fleesha the Futurist.

The house behind the pine tree was Fleesha's house, and Fleesha came to stay in it sometimes, she said, in order to commune with nature.

I would have thought Fleesha could have had all the nature she needed in Amos, but she said, no, ever since her clientele had grown so large she was not able to be easy in Amos. She was able to be easy in Dogtown where there was nothing except the oasis of pine trees surrounded by diggings and the ghosts of the original Dogtown settlers. Not, Fleesha said, that she thought anyone had actually died in Dogtown. The ghosts were those of the settlers' enterprise and of their determination.

Fleesha had made this speech while standing on the edge of our campfire circle, her plump hands clasped, the fire lighting the underside of her double chin and her glasses. She wore men's boots and a dark coat and had a scarf around her ears like a Russian peasant. Now she moved into the circle and sat down on a log, with the boots together. "There is an interesting feeling here," she told us, "the fire is lovely; I am glad to be back in Dogtown."

None of us said anything.

"I am about to build a fire myself," she said. "In my stove."

Sybil said to me, "I hope she burns the house down."

Fleesha heard her. I remembered from my session in Amos that Fleesha had excellent hearing. "I won't burn the house down," she said mildly; "the stove works; I have used it before. It gives a cheery and comforting blaze. And within a few days I will invite you to have a glass of port at my hearth."

Sybil made a noise in her throat. Fleesha rose, pulling her dark coat together, and said, "Good night. I am glad to have you as neighbors," and plodded off toward her house, where, shortly, we saw the glow in the window that meant she had indeed built her fire.

Sybil said, "I am cold, Grace; this has dispirited me. I need to go to bed."

Sybil was jealous; in spite of the fact that she used to be an admirer of Fleesha's she didn't want her there. And I, too, was jealous, angry about the loss of our extra house. But yet as I helped Sybil up, I thought that Fleesha was in some way right in Dogtown; her Russian scarf and round glasses and talk about the ghosts of the pioneer enterprise went with the landscape.

David traveled into Comstock for groceries the next day and came back with the *San Francisco Chronicle;* the paper had a story about Congressman Shaughnessey and the Save America Committee. People in the Congressman's office were to be subpoenaed.

"I wonder what Steve will do." I thought about the greatest good being in betraying your best friend.

"He might do anything. He'll see how he feels when he gets on the stand."

I imagined Steve's precise, specifically enunciated diction saying things about Communism in the California small town and about Daddy's four Socialist pamphlets. "Please let's go for a walk."

We set out for South Fork. After a while David said,

"The water was freezing the last time we were here. Do
you want to go in?"

"Might as well."

"Might as well what?"

"No, I don't want to."

"Steve used to like Jerry Shaughnessey," I said.

Steve had also liked Jesus and the miners. We had had a
discussion about them, about Jesus and the miners, when I
was twelve years old. I had said they were corny, and
Steve, handsome in his blue uniform, had told me corny
expressed nothing, expressed vapidity, expressed a
boughten attitude.

"Oh, hell, David, it's not just that I used to love him, but
didn't he used to be different?"

"Sometimes he was, and sometimes he wasn't."

After we had walked a while longer I said, "I love *you*
now, and not him." This was the first time I had told
David this.

We walked some more, and when we came to a sheltered place we sat down. David lay on his back and pulled
me down, and it seemed public and strange, with the light
rising around us from the white floor of the diggings.

That night Fleesha invited us into her house. We sat on
cushions in front of her iron stove and drank port out of
painted glasses that Fleesha had brought from Amos; she
said they were antiques.

Fleesha understood about the story-telling without having it explained. She began by talking about her gift, which
had happened to her for the first time in Weinstock's in
Sacramento, when she had understood that an elevator
was stuck. The store management had not known about
the elevator, and there was a woman on it who had had

heart attacks and who was starting to breathe erratically by the time the repair crew arrived. "It wasn't," Fleesha said, "that a message came to me, not at all, I just had this urge; I had to go over to the elevator panel and look at it. It was like being thirsty and going to get a glass of water. It was not mysterious."

"It *seems* mysterious," I said.

Fleesha said it seemed mysterious to her when she thought about it or read books about it, but not when it was happening.

Sybil offered to tell a story about living in Pacific Grove with her second husband and eating dinner every night with a Portuguese fisherman's family.

I said, "Fleesha, you understand we don't want people to know we're here."

Fleesha said, "You're my clients. I never talk about my clients' affairs."

It was exactly the right answer, but I could see that Sybil still didn't like it. "Tell us about Pacific Grove, I didn't know you lived in Pacific Grove. Is that where you learned to make paella?"

Sybil said I was pronouncing it wrong. They had had fresh fish every night for a year, she told us, when she lived with the fisherman's family.

"Have you ever found anything lost?" I asked Fleesha.

"Many times." Her voice sounded satisfied.

"The future," I asked. "What happens with the future?"

"That is less clear. Like being thirsty. It is harder to cross the mind-matter boundary into the future."

"Tell us about the things you've found."

The things Fleesha found were jewelry and watches and were not interesting. There was a will that had been hidden in the back of a chimney. I asked, was there ever ten thousand dollars in the refrigerator and Fleesha said, no, but there had been some telephone company stock in a flour bin. She described the flour bin, yellow with a blue decal, and then said, not leading up to it, "I do not like to deal in blood."

"Blood remains," she went on. "It is hard to eradicate. It has a heavy, permeating quality."

That night I asked David, "What does she know?"

"She told us. She knows nothing. She feels antsy."

"Thirsty was what she said." I was uncomfortable about the thirstiness, especially connected with blood. "Why did she come here?"

"She lives here."

"I won't be able to go to sleep."

David put his arms around me and cradled me from behind. "Pretend we're on a boat."

"Will we ever, do you think?"

"Maybe."

"Have you been on a boat?"

He laughed. "Just on Lake Shasta." And he told me about how the editorial board of his school newspaper had rented a Lake Shasta houseboat for a weekend. When he stopped talking I said again, "Does Fleesha know something?" and he said, "She doesn't know what she knows," and I said, "I can't bear being uncertain."

24

The next morning while Sybil was in bed and David off in
Comstock I hiked into French Ford.

There are always hiding places in a neighborhood where
you have lived as a child. I had no plan for what I was
going to do in French Ford, just some general ideas—I
wanted to see my father's high-wheeled Jeep with its medical license plate; I wanted to see Evva from a distance:
brown curly hair and wide skirt; maybe I would settle just
for seeing her rock house.

I thought of my poem about being a ghost in French
Ford.

When I came to the top of Deep Creek Road I hid in the
grove of trees closest to town. Three of the spruce trees had
grown together and had made a cavern between them. I
crawled into this tree house and pulled branches across the
opening. A cloud of pine-scented particles rose in the
bright blue cold sunshine; the town road, twenty feet
above me, shone red dust and asphalt; the asphalt smell
leaked down to me. There was no one on the road. I lay

flat and looked up at an angle and could see the front of the General Store and the gas pump where Lenny Barr had died. Haze rose above the gas pumps. After an hour a brown-haired woman whom I couldn't identify went into the General Store. And then she came out and the road was silent, the red dust settling.

Finally I crawled backwards from the tree house and took a deep breath and dashed across Main Street. I did this at the place beyond the store where the road turned the corner. Then I had to sneak by the back of the firehouse, and after that I was in the trees again.

I skirted the east border of town, up to Mrs. Farmer's house. It looked just the same, the curtains behind the closed windows clean and starched. I sat down next to a wild rosebush and put my hands around my knees.

I was sitting that way when Steve came walking through the field.

He stopped and stared down at me and said, "Hello, Grace; long time no see." He looked tired, bent a little; his pale hair fading into gray, the sun-smear around him gray, too. "What are you doing here?" he asked.

I said, "If you were on foot and I were in a car I would run right over you."

The pale Steve waited, sunlight uncertain around him. I said, "You leave terrible scars."

After a minute he said, "I know I do." Then he walked off.

He seemed to be going toward my father's house. I called out, "Don't go to Dr. Dowell's; there's a man there who reads Communist books."

Before I left French Ford I scribbled a note to Evva and put it under the back door of the telephone exchange. I was taking a chance going up to the exchange building to post the note, but I thought one more chance wouldn't matter.

Back in Dogtown I climbed into my sleeping bag. David found me there. "I can't tell you what's the matter," I said.

"Congressman Shaughnessey is in the papers again," David told me. "This columnist says the Congressman was led astray by the lure of Socialism. The Congressman's office is a bastion of it, the article says."

"What's a bastion?"

"Something like a bulwark."

I curled tighter, and David sat beside me and rubbed my neck. "Maybe you'd better get up. It's not good lying here in the dark."

When I was sitting up he said, "There's no news about Lenny's murder. Nothing for two weeks."

"We're just waiting," I said. "As if we were locked in a closet and told to wait."

"Were you ever locked in a closet?"

"No, never." It surprised me to think of this as a real event that could actually happen.

That afternoon David and I hiked to the South Fork and went swimming. The South Fork was cold and not deep, but you could have a wonderful swim if you traveled with the current, the water fast and buoyant and the banks racing by. Coming back was difficult but it made you feel good.

After dinner we sat by the fire. Fleesha came and talked interestingly about prescience in animals. She didn't like cats, she said, but there was no doubt that cats were prescient; she told us about a cat that knew an earthquake was coming and a cat that had saved a dog's life. This last cat didn't even like the dog; the cat was simply acting as a messenger. After the dog got its foot freed from the railroad tie the cat went back to stealing the dog's food.

I asked Fleesha what color cat and she said black and white, very anonymous. And what color dog? The dog was brown, a brown setter; you like to know the details, don't you? she asked. And I said, it helps me to visualize.

"Your father is like that, too." This was a surprise. I had forgotten that she knew Daddy.

It was a nice evening. David and I went back to the Bar and I fell asleep without any trouble.

Two more days passed that were not memorable, and on the third day it happened.

We had all been expecting something, not knowing what it would be, and I had been dreaming about it. I had dreamed that men in World War II uniforms arrived by parachute. The sky was full of them, slowly floating down. They were Nazi officers, and wore that distinctive hat with the bill.

I was at the North Fork, filling the canvas water bucket that David had bought in Comstock, when I looked out across the diggings, and there, at the crest of the rise that went away from Dogtown toward French Ford, was a cloud of dust. It was spiralling up from a winking object that signalled light. I put the water bucket down. There was no point in running away.

The winking object got larger and looked as if it might be the windshield of a car. After I had decided that this was true I continued to sit, feeling almost composed.

The object winked and heaved and made dust clouds

and grew and became attached to Steve's car, Steve's red car with someone in it. The person in the car had a haze of gray light around his head. I kept on sitting.

The red car stopped on the other side of the North Fork and Steve and I looked at each other. He called out, "Can I get over?"

I pointed to the place where some of the rocks had been spaced on the riverbed in a double row that would fit a pair of tires. The rest of the riverbed was uneven and might upset a small car.

Steve drove slowly across, the water splashing over his tires. I stared at the cap of light around his head and seemed to be feeling nothing much.

He pulled the car up beside me. It was wet halfway up to its doors and fenders; then there was a line of white dust, and the top part of the car still shone bright red.

We stared at each other, Steve in his white leather bucket seat, I wearing jeans and an old sweater and sitting on the ground. I wondered if we were going to remain like that. Maybe this is why he drove the car across the ford, I thought, so he can sit above me, surrounded by a gray haze, and look down. But then he climbed out of the car and squatted nearby, but not too close.

He was wearing working clothes. There were dark streaks under his eyes. He clasped his hands around his knees and looked at the backs of the knuckles. Finally he said, "I'm here with bad news, Grace. Your dad. He's had a heart attack."

I said, "No. No, he hasn't."

I stopped looking at Steve's face, gray, with all the lines going down, and stared instead at the horizon. Steve said, "They've got him in Placer County General."

I thought of times at the Deep Sink, when I had dived too deep and was fighting to come up.

"They're planning to operate."

I watched Steve and thought, There is no way I will ever get rid of you. With your gray face and your treasons. I put my head on my knees. I didn't expect to cry, and I didn't do so.

"Someone is coming," Steve said.

I thought he meant from behind us, either David or Sybil, but when I raised my head I saw that something was traveling across the diggings again, another winking windshield light and a column of dust.

I said, "My God, you led them to us," and stood up.

The shape in the diggings grew larger and became a high-sitting vehicle, probably a Jeep; it made a wide, rolling dust-column. The car seemed to have two people in it. This time I turned around and started to run.

I ran only a little way toward the trees. Then I stopped because, really, there was no place to run to. David and Sybil were coming toward us. They paused as soon as they got out of the trees, and David put his hands halfway up, palms facing forward. I thought, *just the way they do in the movies.*

The two men climbed over the door of their Jeep. I knew only one of them, Kennedy Boggs, Sheriff for Northern Placer County.

"Morning, Mrs. Dowell," he said to Sybil, and "Morning, Grace," to me. Then he added, "Morning, Mrs. Fleesha," and I realized that Fleesha had joined us. She stood with her arms folded and her hands up her sleeves. She looked sad. I was able to feel surprise that Fleesha looked sad.

Sheriff Boggs wore brown army pants and a leather jacket; the man with him, whom I didn't know, was in a brown business suit. "Morning," this man said uninflectedly.

For a while everyone just stood there.

Finally Sheriff Boggs sighed. "That's all right then, Duke; put your hands down. Duke, I got to caution you and read you your rights."

David put down his hands.

"Duke, anything you say may be held against you. You got the right to consult a lawyer."

David said, "Yes."

Sheriff Boggs turned to his companion. "Guess we don't need handcuffs."

"Guess not."

"Which is a good thing, since we don't have any."

I wasn't fooled by this apparent friendliness. That was the way we did things in Placer County. The cheerfulness didn't mean the action wasn't serious.

Steve sat in his red car. He leaned forward, intent. His lips were curved upward as if in amusement; that was how Steve showed interest in something. His arm rested easily along the top of the car door.

Suddenly I couldn't stand that relaxed and graceful arm, those curled fingers holding nothing.

"Steve," I said, "do you remember what you said to Indiana?"

He looked at me; he was grayer now, and not amused. "*What* thing I said to Indiana?"

"You said, 'Indiana. You mean nothing to me.' "

He moved his shoulders. He stared at me, the pupils of his eyes getting small.

231

"I don't know," I said. "I was going to say that to you. Now I don't want to.

"It suddenly came to me," I went on, "that if I keep on hating you it will kill me. It will kill my soul and wither it away into a scrap."

David and the two men were still facing each other calmly, easy and indigenous, like a group of McCrackens around the General Store gas pump. Sybil moved up, crippled-looking, and put her arms around David from behind and said, "I've always loved you."

Behind me Steve's car started. It made reversing noises too fast: the tires screaming for traction, screeching backward twice, then forward twice. There was a splash as the wheels and front bumper hit the water.

I turned to watch. Steve was driving too fast, the carriage rocking and sending up sprays of water.

In midstream the car wavered; its wheels veered first right and then left.

Steve twisted the steering wheel; the car bucked and squealed as if the carriage had locked; he tugged at the wheel again. And slowly, a giant hand under water seeming to push it, the car began to turn over.

Sheriff Boggs said, "Hi," and "Hey." Sybil said, "Oh, dear God." David started running.

I didn't say anything. I stood, my feet attached to the quartz diggings rock. Deliberately, the car moved, first onto its side; I could see Steve still clutching the wheel. And then, deliberately, one more turn, water swirling around it, wheels revolving rapidly, it stopped, upside down. Gray-green current grabbed at the muddy undercarriage; water washed the still-revolving wheels. Steve had disappeared underneath.

We waded into the stream and pulled at metal edges. Everyone did this, even Sibyl. I got my hand under something. In a frozen moment all sensation seemed to have stopped; the five people were not talking; water congealed at our feet; the sky hung, high and black; there were no birds. My hands, which ought to have been hurting, clenched and tugged and had no feeling.

"This way, Jim," Sheriff Boggs said, "easy now, *easy*. She's caught on a rock. Grace, step back; Grace, get your goddamn hand outta there; Grace, step back."

I did and the car went over.

Steve lay, half on his side. His body looked unplanned, unorganized, a flung sweater, arms and legs splayed, mouth ajar. One eye was open and staring up. A snail's trail of blood stained his cheek from ear to chin.

Sheriff Boggs put his hand under Steve's head and turned him to get the face out of water. The right cheek was scraped, blood oozed.

The sheriff bent to listen. Then he picked up a wrist.

The shallow water swirled. It had soaked through Steve's clothes; it was drowning the lower half of him.

The sheriff and the business-suited man wrestled Steve out of the car and onto the round shore rocks. The rest of us followed; I sat down on the rocks; I gripped my hands around my knees. A few details seemed clear: the business-suited man's pants were wet halfway up; Steve's hands flopped. Like flower heads, I thought foolishly, like heavy flower heads. The sheriff bent over, felt the side of Steve's throat. Finally he turned to us and shook his head.

"He's dead." In case we hadn't understood.

David asked, "Can I go to her?" and the sheriff said, "Yeah."

233

David leaned over me.

My shoes were oozing water. I started trying to untie them.

"Don't, Grace," David said. "Don't, darling; don't."

It took me a while to realize that he wasn't talking about my shoes but about the noise I was making. And it took a while longer to recognize the noise. It was the same one Sybil had described Daddy making when he lay beside my mother, the crying of an injured animal.

David finally got me to be quiet by kneeling behind me and putting his hands on my shoulders.

25

"Daddy," I said, "Daddy. Oh, my God, I'm so glad you didn't die."

"Not to dwell on it." My father was home. He was in his four-poster bed, the same one, I supposed, that my mother had died in. (I had often thought this, but had never asked anybody about it.) Daddy was pale; his eyes were circled and he still wore his plastic hospital wristband. "Hey, Babe"—he sounded surprised and pleased—"you were really worried . . . shouldn't worry about your old dad."

"You should have told me."

"Aw, honey, why bug you? I mean, all that grief?"

"You *ought* to have."

He sighed. "I guess I do treat you like a kid."

"Yes."

"How old *are* you?"

"I'm twenty."

"You had a birthday . . ." I'd had a birthday when no

one, least of all me, could pay any attention to it. My father said, "Babe . . . I'm really sorry about Steve."

"Be sorry about David. David's innocent; David was set up; he didn't do anything; he was a victim . . ."

I sat for a while, my hands locked in my lap; then Daddy reached and took the thumb that was sticking up out of the locked hands, and I let go and grabbed onto him.

He said, "Maybe you'll have a hard time mourning Steve."

"Steve? It's David."

"Steve did some pretty strange things. Maybe you wished bad luck for him."

I got up and walked to the window. Daddy's room was bigger than mine and had floor-to-ceiling windows with blue-striped curtains. I stuck my head through them and looked out; here it was again in my view—French Ford and its tin roofs, now with melting snow. I said, "I hate psychiatry."

"Sorry, Babe."

"And I hate . . ." I was going to say that I hated being called Babe, but stopped myself. Daddy had been calling me that all my life; he couldn't go back now and change all those words; he probably couldn't even stop saying Babe now. I dropped the curtain-edge and went back to my chair.

"It was mostly that it was so sudden." I meant Steve's death.

Daddy took my hand again.

"And nothing was settled." This didn't seem to make sense, so I tried some more. "I mean, everything was the same, except Steve was dead." And this last formulation made no sense at all.

"Listen, Daddy." Now I was starting a new, difficult subject. "I promised myself I'd tell you. I think you've been a good father. I know it was hard. You had this sullen, smart-alec child . . ." I clutched his hand tightly. "I just realized. You must have felt *lonely*."

All the while I was saying this I kept thinking, underneath, about Steve. I had promised myself I wouldn't grieve for Steve. He was dead. When you were dead, you were dead. Steve was weird; Evva was right; now he lay close to Indiana, close enough to reach out and touch her. He lay there with all those issues unsettled.

But the next week I found out that something, at least, had been settled.

The man who came to see me looked generally familiar, as if he were a type I had known, or seen in the movies, or read about. He had smooth tan hair, a hard-finished blue suit, and his eyes looked at me unemotionally and then shifted to stare at the air by my ear. "Miss Dowell?" he said.

"I'm Mrs. McCracken."

"Oh. Yes . . . May I come in?"

Part of me didn't want to talk to this man and part of me did. I unhooked the screen and led the way to the front room.

When he was seated on a petit-point chair with the light on his face, I realized who he looked like: he resembled the business-suited cop from the day Steve died. But he wasn't the same person, just a similar one. He handed me a card.

JOHN FOWLER
Research Aide
SAVE AMERICA

237

"Miss . . . Mrs. McCracken. We are conducting an inquiry. There were some questions left unanswered." He cleared his throat. "Because of your cousin's unfortunate death."

I was silent. After a while he asked, "Who is Grazia?"

When I still didn't say anything he went on, in a monotone, "We thought it might be you. Because Grazia is the Spanish form of Grace."

He seemed pleased with himself about this, so I said, "Italian. Not Spanish. Italian."

"Oh. Yes." He waited for a while. "We have a document," he said.

"A what?"

He pulled a single sheet of paper from his briefcase.

"A letter?" I asked.

"Not exactly. You see, there was to have been . . ."

I dulled my hearing for the next sentences. ". . . helping us with our investigations . . . a patriotic gesture . . ."

"Steve was going to testify for you?"

"He said he had material . . ." Aide Fowler creased his egg-smooth forehead. "He said it might *amuse* us. A curious phrase."

When I didn't answer he muttered, "Well," and fiddled with the sheet of paper. I finally asked, "Do you mean Steve wrote to me?" and he said, "Not exactly," and, after a pause, handed the paper over.

It wasn't, strictly speaking, a letter. It was headed *MEMO.*

MEMO
To: Grazia
From: Jean Genet
Subject: Action; Inaction

238

The acte gratuit *is kind of a bore, after all.*
    The acte gratuit
    May not be
    The mode for me
    It lacks esprit
    The hell with these damn rhymes; they bore me too; I'm
going off to Afghanistan with my camel.

"He didn't send us any documents," Aide Fowler said.
"Just that."

"It doesn't tell you much, does it?"

"We thought you might clarify."

"I think it's a joke. Steve liked jokes."

The aide cleared his throat.

Well, you'll never find out now, will you? I said to myself. Aide Fowler stared at my eyes and then at my ear.
"Goodbye," he said, "thank you; we appreciate your co-
operation." I wanted to tell him, I didn't cooperate, Mis-
ter, but kept quiet and watched him exit through the
screen door, carrying his piece of paper with him.

"His *camel*," Evva said, "what in hell did he mean,
Afghanistan with his camel; was he going to take up camel
buggering; oh, for Christ's sake, don't *cry*."

"It proves it, doesn't it, he didn't kill himself?"

"God. Have you been worrying about *that*? Listen, just
tell me, how can somebody turn their car over *on purpose*
in the middle of the North Fork? And stop crying."

I wasn't crying, I told her.

We had buried Steve in the wintertime, so he didn't get a
mat of electric green grass; his was a puffy white snow

239

mat, suitable for winter burials. And I had looked down on it and thought, oh, Jesus, how he would have hated this, being put in the cold ground under a white fur bath mat. And I hadn't cried then, either. Steve's mother cried; she had done the crying for the whole town of French Ford.

26

Evva is helping me pack. She sits cross-legged on the floor, wearing blue jeans and an old white shirt of Lloyd's, and throws clothes either toward the wastebasket or toward my suitcase.

"I might as well get some good out of it," she says, meaning Lloyd's white shirt, "he's not going to be wearing it for a while."

They found Lloyd in Truckee three days after David was arrested; Argo turned up last week in Sacramento. Buddy is still *at large,* as the sheriff puts it.

"Bunch of jerks," Evva says, "why do they have to stick so close to home?" I say, "Well, why did *I?*" and Evva agrees, "Okay, why?" but doesn't pursue the question. She understands pretty well why.

Evva's the ideal person to help me pack; she's quick and decisive. And sporadically, because she is also neat, she crawls on hands and knees to my suitcase and folds things professionally, sweater sleeves inside the body of the sweater.

"How long will Lloyd get off for good behavior?" she asks. "If he's good."

"He'll be good."

Lloyd and David were sentenced last month, Lloyd to four years, David to only one. The judge and the lawyers looked embarrassed about David; no one, it appeared, really thought he was involved in the actual shooting, but no one could prove that he wasn't, either.

I tell Evva, "We both need some vodka."

Mrs. Farmer is in the kitchen scrubbing shelves. "Can I help you, lovey?"

I say no and climb the ladder for the vodka. Anything I say to Mrs. Farmer these days seems like a rejection and anything she says to me like an apology. Because it was Mrs. Farmer who, going down Main Street at midnight to bring water to Hattie the horse, saw Lenny Barr die and saw that David was there. "I kept quiet for a while, Grace, and that was wrong. I had to say about David."

From the stepladder I watch Mrs. Farmer's fluffed white hair. She is right to be meek with me; I hated her for a while. I collect vodka glasses and ice and push the stepladder under the shelf and go back upstairs thinking about the last months and the blur they make. I don't exactly hate Mrs. Farmer any more; she's just part of a general heavy feeling of this time; she couldn't help it; what did I expect, people to be different from what they are?

"If Lloyd is good," I hand Evva her glass, "really good, he'll get two years off."

"You think so, honest?"

"Honest."

We clink glasses to Lloyd's two years. Evva is sitting in the window seat now, with one foot up and her back to the pane. Her eyes are deep-circled and she has lost weight; all this only makes her look prettier; the circles are a good color—purple, like eye makeup.

Evva and I are going to live together in Sacramento. Evva will go to nursing school and I'm not sure what I will do.

"Evva," I say, "why do I keep dreaming about Steve?"

"Do you?"

"Yes."

"Well, stop."

"That's great advice; listen, if you think it's as easy as that . . ."

Of the people I have lost, it is Steve whom I dream about.

Steve comes to the house in my dream—not my French Ford house, perhaps Mrs. Sanchez's house; he brings an assortment of battered, empty cardboard boxes. What, I ask him, hurt, what does he think I want with this tattered useless trash? He stares at me with his needy Steve look. I am washing dishes; he leans on the edge of the sink.

Steve and a woman wearing a red scarf drive away from me into Diaspora Mine. I watch the backs of their heads and the rounded back of the car with its black and orange license plate for longer than it should be possible to see a car disappearing into a tunnel. They know that I am watching, but they don't look back.

Steve's dead face and splayed body lie on the mattress on the floor of Mrs. Sanchez's Aqua Room. One hand clutches the collar of Sybil's pink jacket.

"Forget it," Evva says. "About your dreams. They're not important. Anyway . . ." she's fishing for words, "they're just a way of saying goodbye."

"Maybe."

"You'll dream and dream and then you'll stop. And be all over that."

We drink silently. I say, "I feel as if I were under water."

"Yes."

"Or buried in a mine." I'm thinking of Diaspora.

Evva starts lecturing in her clipped psychiatry voice, the one that goes with reading the psychiatry section of her nurse's textbook. "It's a defense. That feeling of being muffled up is a defense. To keep you from hurting too much."

"I have trouble remembering what David looked like."

"A defense." She gets a whole ice cube in her teeth and crunches it. "Try. Try again to remember."

I do, and something happens—first, I see the bottom of David's thin face, and then the part of it that includes the brown eyes with their long upturned lashes; recollection returns like bits of a jigsaw puzzle. Evva is watching me.

"See?"

I am still trying to remember David's nose. And after a while I've recovered his whole, vulnerable, loving face, and then I remember how Sybil came up to him and held him and told him she had always loved him. I say, "Evva, you're my best friend."

"Well, I always was your best friend; there's nothing new in that. Why in *hell* do you buy knit cotton underwear?" She holds a pair of underpants up by their elastic. "They look as if they ought to be . . . Sybil's."

But I tell her she's absolutely wrong; Sybil likes silk, imported silk.

* * *

"David," I say, "hey, David, I've *got* to stick with you. I've got to have that baby that's half McCracken and half Dowell, remember?"

It's hard, sometimes, to keep these conversations light. Maybe that's a mistake. Maybe they're not supposed to be light.

We are in the Visitor's Room of Jefferson Correctional Facility. The Visitor's Room is painted chocolate brown up to shoulder height; above that it is hospital green; lengthwise the room is divided by a gray plastic counter with a mesh partition above it. On one side of the partition sits a row of men in blue denim work clothes; on the other side is Us, the visitors, mostly women, a few men, some children. There are more of us than of them because some prisoners have several visitors, who wait their turn on the sidelines in gray metal chairs.

I keep watching for signs that David is changing. So far he seems about the same.

We are allowed to hold hands under the mesh. I stick my hand under, palm up. He puts his hand over mine; I look at our two conjoined hands.

"Why are you not living with your husband?" Sybil asked me yesterday. "Young people who are just married should live together."

When I told her David was in jail she said, "Oh. That makes a difference."

Sybil is still in her automobile in the diggings. Daddy tried to get her to move into town with him, but she refused. He says he expects to come out there some morning and find her dead of exposure, and I think, maybe that's what will happen. It seems like an all right way to go.

"I brought you some books." I hold them up. They'll have to pass through inspection before he gets them.

David actually looks well. He's tan, and the blue cover-all uniform suits him.

I suppose they check the books to make sure they aren't hollow, with a weapon or a bomb or money inside them.

"Should I be living with Daddy?" I ask him. "Do you think Daddy's lonely?"

A quiver goes through our conjoined hands under the mesh barrier; David's fingers tighten. Of course it's the word *lonely* that has done this. David, you're not lonely; that's not the word for it in this heavy-breathing army of blue-shirted, blue-jeansed men. I try to imagine the long regimented days: the line-up for breakfast, for lunch, for dinner, for exercise. For the bathroom? I've read some-where that there is a toilet for each cell, but I don't ask David about this. He'd tell me, though; it wouldn't embar-rass him; he doesn't mind talking about the details of his life. David, my darling. You are good and frank; you are free, even if you are in jail.

"You shouldn't be living with your dad," David says gently. "He understands that. Don't worry about it." We squeeze fingertips.

"How much longer?" I say. "How many days?"

"Three hundred and twenty-seven."

"You'll get time off for good behavior."

Evva and I have each started keeping a big calendar to mark off the passage of time. Evva uses stars to mark hers, a star for each day that's passed. I started out with X's but that began to seem too negative; now I draw pictures: a sun or a tree for all-right days, rain clouds for bad ones.

Once there was a volcano for a day when I threw a pillow at Evva.

Evva goes to see Lloyd on the third Friday of each month. Lloyd is in Tyler, which is higher security than Jefferson. "But it's all right," Evva says, "he's learning auto mechanics."

I look at David and remember that he believes in the brotherhood of man. David says it is okay here, really. Word has gone out that he wouldn't talk about his brothers, and the other convicts like that.

"If you've done something to a child," he tells me, "you have a hard time in jail."

I stare down at our conjoined hands and remember the nights in Dogtown when I curled up because of the cold, and David curved behind me spoon-fashion. I say, "I think of you at night; it helps to think of you at night," and he says, "Yes."

The schoolbell over the clock rings. It goes for about twenty seconds. David and I squeeze hands under the mesh: then I stand up and put my lips against the screen. The kiss is mostly metal and rust, but between those tastes I can feel a little of David's lips. "Goodbye, darling," I say, and David says, "Goodbye, darling."

The sergeant goes down the line tapping prisoners on the shoulder. David gets up, looks at me, turns, walks away. His shoulders are too stiff. I call after him, "Thursday the sixteenth," and he moves his head.

I take the books to the sergeant at the door, and then I walk to the bus.

Half the women on the return bus are always crying. It makes for a community of feeling.

I am thinking of the poem about the man of double deed, the poem that I attach to Steve.

Evva says, "Sure, it's unfair. Life is unfair. But would you rather have David dead? Steve is *dead*."

I still dream about Steve.

I say to Evva, "It says in the poem, 'When the seed began to grow/It made a summer full of snow.'"

Evva says, "Bullshit. David's not in jail because of Steve. He's in jail because he followed his brothers down to the General Store. He feels guilty because he couldn't stop them."

"Evva, do you think we'll ever live in French Ford again?"

"No. French Ford is different now."

For a while I thought that the true French Ford, the one that kept on the way French Ford used to be, was Dogtown. But then Evva found a story in the *Bee* that said the Forest Service had knocked Dogtown down, all five houses of it, because vagrants were living in them.

Fleesha didn't own her house in Dogtown; no one could own those houses because title to them had been lost.

I didn't tell David about this. When someone is in jail they don't like to hear that a place they love has been destroyed.

But after thinking about it I decided maybe it was for the best. It meant that no one could ever take Dogtown away from us. It belonged to us only, at least in memory.

The bus has started; I put my face near the open window and smell the dust and tar and think about those same smells on a hot summer day in French Ford. First I remember Steve in French Ford, and then myself there alone, and then me and Steve, and finally a little bit of myself with David.

I have again my vision of French Ford as a paperweight, an elegantly detailed and precise one, containing our house, the store, the graveyard, and all the eccentric and innocent people. I can look into the heart of the globe and see the firehouse door come up, the woman in a print dress appear on Indiana's porch, and all the beginning of that train of events that seemed to start with Indiana's death but that really had commenced much earlier, maybe as far back as the four original Dowells.

The woman next to me asks if I want half a sandwich. It's the wrong kind of sandwich; limp white bread and bright orange cheese and wilted lettuce, but I accept it gratefully.

"I was watching you with your boyfriend," she says. "The two of you are so sweet together."

I don't tell her that I am going to embroider this on a sampler. I settle back with my head in the corner of the bus window and think about the baby who will be half McCracken and half Dowell. That child is going to have all the qualities that are needed.

Diana O'Hehir is an award-winning poet and the author of the critically acclaimed novel *I Wish This War Were Over*. She teaches English and creative writing at Mills College in Oakland, California.